LITERARY OUTLAW

A PULP FICTION MAGAZINE | ISSUE #5

IN THIS ISSUE:

LITERARY OUTLAW #5
Copyright © 2024 by LiteraryOutlawLLC

Front Cover - Bodleian Library, Oxford engraving (modified) | Public Domain
Legendarium | Copyright © 2014 by Michael Bunker & Kevin G. Summers
Page 21 - Cheshire Cat by John Tenniel | Public Domain
Cassandra | Public Domain. Art by Don Heck & Mike Esposito.
Originally published in *Psycho #14*
The Comet | Public Domain. Originally published *Darkwater: Voices From Within the Veil, 1920*
The Woman In The Mirror | Public Domain. Originally published *Black Magic #1*
Penrod | Public Domain. Originally published in 1914
A Trap for Nemesis | Public Domain. Originally published in *The Ghost Rider #1*
The Hollow Men | Public Domain. Originally published in *Eliot's Poems: 1909–1925*
The Mask | Public Domain. Originally published in *The King in Yellow, 1895*
Moby Dick | Public Domain. Originally published in *Thriller Comics Library $157*

The stories in this magazine are works of fiction. Names, characters, businesses, places, events and incidents are either the products of the author's imagination or used in a fictitious manner. Any resemblance to actual persons, living or dead, or actual events is purely coincidental.

All rights reserved. This book or any portion thereof may not be reproduced or used in any manner whatsoever without the express written permission of the publisher except for the use of brief quotations in a book review.

www.literaryoutlaw.com

LEGENDARIUM

BY MICHAEL BUNKER & KEVIN G. SUMMERS

PROLOGUE:
HUGH HOWEY MUST LIVE

HUGH HOWEY WAS HUNGRY. THE *New York Times* bestselling author used a bony finger to scan the books on his luncheon tray, but he had trouble deciding exactly what he wanted to eat. Nabokov again? Nah, how many times a week can you eat Nabokov? There was some O'Henry here and a book of Chekhov plays… those looked good. Ahh, here was Henry James's *Travel Writings*. He picked up the volume and sniffed it. Delicious. A literary/culinary delight that would satisfy him perfectly until the evening meal. As he opened the book, ripped out a page, and shoved it into his mouth, he was just thinking that for supper he'd have some Neil Gaiman, or perhaps he'd dip into that A.G. Riddle book that was storming the charts.

Hugh hadn't seen his friend Bombo Dawson since they'd parted at the airport in London back in January. That was after the two authors had saved England—and probably the whole world—from an infestation of zombies that ate only good writers. He thought back on that crazy time with a bittersweet mixture of sadness and nostalgia. The two men had raced—well, walked briskly; it was still more than enough to leave Bombo gasping for breath—through London's darkened streets during the height of the zombie infestation, being chased by thousands of writers-turned-zombies.

Luring the zombies to the Tower of London had been simple enough. The zombies were all former writers—good, talented writers—who'd been infected with a virus that caused them to want to attack and consume other good authors. These undead scribes were the product of a British military experiment gone horribly awry. So Bombo and Hugh had been used as bait, to lure the biters to their *re-death*.

The ploy was as implausible as it was farfetched, and had been designed by some mid-level pencil-pushing wonk who hadn't slept in two days, but ultimately it was successful… at least, mostly so. Unhappily, in the midst of the mission, *New York Times* bestselling author and all-around great guy Hugh Howey had been scratched on his leg by the zombie formerly known as Sue Grafton.

Now, he was mostly zombie-ish. Mostly.

He wasn't *all* the way dead. At least, not yet. His transformation from unassuming author to unassuming undead zombie was moving along painfully slowly. He'd only just begun to stink. And Bella, his dog, had started to chew on his fingers and toes a bit now and then.

He'd received such a low dosage of the virus from the undead Sue Grafton that his body had, so far, been able to fight it off. So, in a way, it was like he had a long-term zombiesque cold. His condition was slowly getting worse, but he was still in the fight.

His wife, along with the lawyers at Simon and Schuster, had decided to chain him to his desk inside his Florida home so he could keep writing—and to keep him away from any well-meaning persons who might choose to smash his brains in with a pitching wedge. And so he wrote; and frankly, his fans couldn't have been happier. His already prolific output had multiplied, which satisfied everyone involved. Sure, he didn't do many unboxing videos anymore. Not since that time when he'd unboxed his *GRIT Omnibus,* and the overwhelmingly delicious smell wafting from the box had caused him to rip into the books hungrily with his teeth, without any thought that he was recording the video to put up on his blog. Nobody wanted to see that.

The bestselling author of *The COTTON Omnibus* also agreed—as a gesture to the memory of Sue Grafton and as a gift to her legions of adoring fans—to ghost-write the next novel in her famous alphabet series. It just so happened that Ms. Grafton had become a zombie before finishing her "W" novel, so Hugh had just put the finishing touches on the next, absolutely and undeniably awesome Sue Grafton title…

"W" is for WOOL

He thought it was catchy. Probably no one else would. What kind of name was that for a book? Sounded like a scouring pad, or a sweater of some sort. Would followers and fans of the book be called "Woolites"? Oh well, in literature, he thought, there was no accounting for taste.

Hugh's "office" was a room in his cozy Florida home near the beach. Though he was chained to the desk, there was a bathroom attached to the office, and when the need happened to arise—even zombies had to go sometimes, and boy,

those John Grisham and Stephanie Meyer novels went straight through him—he could use the bathroom. His chain was just—long—enough.

The bathroom was mostly unspectacular, but it did have ceramic tile and a claw foot bathtub in case he had a particularly sweaty day of writing. Now, as he tore out another delicious page from Henry James's *Travel Writings,* the door to that bathroom swung open, seemingly of its own accord.

Hugh felt the hunger pains grow worse as a hooded figure emerged from the bathroom. Well, maybe not *from the bathroom* so much as *from a glowing, ethereal light that glowed forth* from the bathroom.

The figure was dressed in white robes and wore atop them a long, white cloak. The figure's face was cast in shadow, but from the rumbling in his gut, Hugh Howey was certain that this was an author of great renown. In fact, he knew that whoever this figure was… he or she would be delicious.

The head tilted slightly and Hugh knew that the figure was sizing him up too. "Are you the international bestselling author Hugh Howey?" said the figure in white. It was a man; there was no sense in pretending otherwise. That's not to say that a woman would be inferior in any way, just that this otherworldly, perhaps magical being, just happened to be a man. okay?

Hugh Howey nodded slowly, his blue eyes fixed on the figure standing before him. The man, who was unusually tall, drew back his hood to reveal a face framed by a mop of blackish-brown curly hair. *Kurt Vonnegut.*

Hugh dropped the book he'd been eating—a tiny piece of one of the pages still bulged from his mouth—and pointed at the specter. "Kurt Vonnegut?" he mumbled. Howey's voice shook a little, and he didn't know whether he should kneel down or genuflect or… you know… offer to give Vonnegut a high-five or something else appropriate like that. He'd seen a lot in his lifetime, but having a dead author—one of his favorites, mind you—step out of his crapper in a glow of heavenly light was unusual to say the least. He could tell right away that Vonnegut was no zombie, but he was still quite dead.

So it goes.

Howey choked down the rest of the page he had in his mouth, and Vonnegut smiled. He looked younger than he had when he'd died back in 2007. As a matter of fact, he looked just like he had in his author photo on the back of *Slaughterhouse-Five*. "This is probably a big surprise to you," Vonnegut said. "God knows, it was a surprise to me when Mark Twain showed up at my house on Cape Cod back in 1971."

"Excuse me?" Howey said.

"Never mind," said Vonnegut. "Close your mouth, son. Being mostly dead, you'll start to attract flies sooner or later, and zombie or no, flies aren't a good part of any diet. Now listen up. I'm here as a representative of the Legendarium. Ever heard of it?"

Hugh closed his mouth and shook his head no.

"Didn't think so," Vonnegut said. "The Legendarium is a library, but not like the one down the street from your house." Vonnegut gazed around the room and then nodded at Hugh. "Say, Hugh, this is a nice house."

"Thanks."

"Anyway, the Legendarium… it's a *metaphysical* library. It exists at the nexus of the multiverse, at the point where all stories intersect."

Hugh nodded his head and then shrugged. "Of course it does."

"Are you being obtuse, Hugh?" Vonnegut asked.

"No, sir," Hugh said. "I'm just sitting here thinking that… *of course* there's a bad-ass super library out there, now that I'm becoming a zombie and can't really visit it." He pulled his chain and rattled it for Vonnegut.

"You'll get to see it someday. I'm sure of it," Vonnegut said.

Hugh shrugged again. "Probably not. Certainly not as long as I'm in this condition."

"I can dig it," Vonnegut said. "But all of that is neither here nor there right now." Vonnegut stuck his hands into the deep pockets of his white cloak. "As I was saying: there exists this… *super library*, as you called it. It exists out there, and every story ever written comes together at that one, critical point, at the nexus of the multiverse. Does that make any sense to you?"

"Not a bit," said Hugh Howey.

"They should've sent C.S. Lewis," Vonnegut grumbled. "He could have explained this better than me. But I wanted to meet you."

"Me?" asked the exceedingly humble bestselling author.

"I read your fanfic," Vonnegut said.

"Oh," said Hugh Howey. He flushed, if such a thing was possible for a zombie. "I… um… Kindle Worlds asked me to write that and…"

"I loved it," Vonnegut said.

"You did?"

"At first I was skeptical about other people using my characters," Vonnegut said. "You know about the whole thing with *Venus On The Half-Shell*, right?"

Hugh Howey nodded.

"But then I read a few of the fanfic stories, and… wow. Your story had me in tears, Hugh." The two authors just stared at one another for a few seconds before Vonnegut took a deep breath and continued. "Anyway, the Legendarium is in trouble, and I've been sent to recruit some authors to defend it."

Hugh looked at the chains binding him to his desk. He thought about the zombie virus that was slowly eating away at him from the inside. He knew he was in no condition to save this Legendarium. "I'm sorry," he said, "but I don't think I can help you."

Vonnegut scowled.

"Besides," Hugh said, "turning me loose in a library right now would be like taking George R.R. Martin to an all-you-can-eat buffet. No one wants to see that."

Vonnegut took a closer look at Hugh Howey, and as he drew nearer, Hugh had to resist the urge to lunge at the great writer. The desire to get a taste of the man who'd written *Slaughterhouse-Five* was overwhelming. He'd really be the *Breakfast of Champions*, Hugh thought to himself. He laughed at his own joke and realized that he was glad that he was chained. He'd never forgive himself if he ate Kurt Vonnegut. He didn't stop to wonder whether one could actually eat a ghost at all.

"You look like something the cat dragged in," Vonnegut said. "What happened to you?"

"It's a long story."

Vonnegut frowned. "Maybe another time. For now, I need a few heroes to save the world. If you can't help us, can you suggest anyone that can? It has to be a writer, and it has to be someone really good. Someone with heft… you know? A serious author with an overwhelming hunger. Someone with literary *gravitas*."

Hugh Howey smiled as he thought of his new friend, Bombo Dawson. He said, "I think I know just the person."

CHAPTER ONE:
THE DRAWING OF THE TWO

BREAKFAST ON THE TERRACE IS A GREAT idea—provided that three, and only three, requisite circumstances are met. First, the weather should be pleasant. That one is a given, and doesn't merit much comment. Second, pests of all kinds—this includes bugs, children, and dogs—should not be present at such an important time. Third (and this was the big one), rules… well… they should be kept to a minimum.

It's just plain un-American, that's what it is, Bombo thought. *Choices shouldn't be this hard, and what kind of person buys a dozen assorted donuts and then tells you that you can only pick one? What kind of thing is that?*

Carol, Bombo Dawson's new wife, had her largish man on a tight leash, gastronomically speaking. She'd completely failed in her attempts to get him to trim his voluminous beard or to shower more often, but she'd insisted that he go on a diet. She was concerned about his weight. *He* wasn't concerned at all about it, but she was. Apparently his performance in the harrowing three-mile chase—from the offices of *The Colonel Magazine* to the Tower of London, while being chased by writer-eating zombies (who had impressive stamina, he'd thought at the time)—caused Carol to be of the opinion that perhaps Bombo wasn't in the best shape of his life. *But who is?* he thought. *I was in the best shape of my life when I was twenty, and since then it's gone downhill. But it's sure been an enjoyable downhill ride.* The thought of now eating only one donut sickened him. *Communism, that's what it is. I've married a communist.*

As if she were reading his thoughts, just then Carol pushed open the sliding glass door and joined her new husband on the terrace. She nonchalantly sprayed him with a can of Febreze, an act that had become something of a ceremony between them. In fact, he'd come to expect it, and he'd even grown to appreciate the *linen and sky* aroma. Like Pavlov's dog, whenever he smelled that particular scent, he knew that Carol was around, and that things were mostly right with the world.

She pointed a finger at Bombo. "Are you going to just stare at them, or are you going to pick one?"

"You're a commie, aren't you, comrade?" he asked.

Carol's jaw dropped. She was used to her husband's eccentricities already, but that didn't stop her from being shocked at the things that came out of his mouth. "What? Bombo? Me, a commie? What are you talking about?"

Bombo narrowed his eyes at Carol and pointed a finger back at her. "Right now, without thinking about it, Carol—just spit out an answer. In which city would you rather live: Volgograd? Or Stalingrad?"

"What? I don't even know what you're asking me, Bombo."

"Ha! Trick question!" the chubby author said. "They're both names for the same city, Carol, and you wanted to say Stalingrad, I could see it in your little pinko eyes. But you knew that if you said Stalingrad, you'd be exposing your communist underbelly!"

Just then, the phone started to ring in the house. Carol's head turned at the sound, and Bombo took advantage of the diversion to grab two donuts: a crème-filled and a chocolate-covered with sprinkles. He'd already swallowed half of the crème-filled donut and was walking by Carol through the still-opened door when Carol began her protest. "Bombo!"

"Don't deny it!" Bombo said, his mouth filled with donut and vanilla crème as he shuffled, surprisingly dexterously, past Carol, "I should have known better than to get a wife in Great Britain. That place is crawling with commies…"

Ding.

"Stop calling me a commie, Bombo!" Carol started to argue but Bombo interrupted her with a chocolate-covered finger stuck in front of her face. "Hold that thought, comrade. My phone just dinged."

Bombo reached into the pocket of his red flannel shirt and produced a device the size of a pocket calculator which contained a computer more sophisticated than the machines used to put a man on the moon. That's assuming, of course, that you believe a man actually walked on the moon. Bombo still wasn't completely sold on that particular notion. He slid a chocolaty finger across the face of his phone and began to read. His body tensed noticeably and Carol took an involuntary step back.

"What is it?" Carol asked, her bellicose tone from moments before evaporating like superheated water.

"Someone just gave a one-star review to *Anne Askew In The Tower*," Bombo said. He blinked back tears as the words of the review twisted in his heart.

"Let me see that," Carol said. She took the phone and read the review. As she was wholly occupied reading, Bombo smiled to himself and moved stealthily to the box of donuts. He took a Boston crème and bit into it without thinking, allowing the combination of chocolate and pastry and vanilla pudding to soothe his troubled spirit.

"Whoever wrote this is a complete wanker," Carol said. "He's probably—hey, are you eating another donut?"

Bombo shoved the rest of the Boston crème into his mouth, spilling a bit of pudding into his beard as he did so. "No," he said with his mouth full.

"Bombo! I'm just worried about your health," Carol said. "You can't keep eating like this and hope to live a good long life. I don't want to be a widow, you know?"

Bombo nodded, swallowing most of the donut in one gulp.

"I've been reading this book about vegan dieting—" Carol began, when something very peculiar happened.

The terrace door opened, spilling blinding light into the Kentucky morning. It was impossible, Bombo knew, but the light coming from the other side of the door was actually brighter than the sun. It took a minute for his eyes to adjust, but when they did, Bombo saw a man in a flowing white robe standing next to the grill. The figure had a long white beard and penetrating eyes. Bombo lowered his cell phone and stared. He'd been licking the chocolate off the screen when the specter had first appeared, which may be why the figure before him was now staring at him with narrowed eyes. Bombo recognized the man at once: it was Leo Tolstoy.

★ ★ ★

THE REVIEW WAS POSTED ON GOODREADS and the critic's personal webpage. It read as follows:

> ★— *Anne Askew In The Tower is the worst piece of crap that I have ever read in my entire life. It's the kind of book that is so hackneyed that you just can't look away. It reads like it was written in one sitting by a redneck high on donuts and cappuccino. And the author,*

> *Bombo Dawson, he looks like a long-lost relative from that show Duck Dynasty. I mean, he makes Patrick Rothfuss and George R.R. Martin appear well-groomed. Whatever you do, don't buy this book. Not even the e-book. Don't get it even if it's free on Kindle Unlimited. I give this book 1-star because they won't let me go into negative numbers. It's that bad.*

The reviewer's name was Alistair Foley. He was a thirty-five-year-old man with thinning hair on top, a ponytail in back, and wrinkles at the edges of his eyes. He had a neatly trimmed mustache and a hoop earring in his left ear. He wore vests and ties and a sports coat, once belonging to his grandfather, with patches on the elbows. He was a creative writing teacher at the community college in his hometown of Carmel, Virginia.

Alistair Foley was also a frequent reviewer of books on the various websites listed above. He had the tendency to give scathing reviews to practically everything he read. He patrolled—or, more properly, *trolled*—literary territory like a shark looking for victims. He enjoyed fantasy and science fiction, but was extremely particular even then. If the author was Martin or Rothfuss or King or Salvatore, his reviews were usually positive. If the book strayed too far away from what he considered to be "high literature" however, more often than not Alistair would fillet the author.

Foley sat at his desk in his empty classroom at the community college. It was lunchtime, and he was enjoying the break between classes by critically shredding Bombo Dawson's literary debut. The book had only been on the market for a few months, and already it had eighty-seven five-star reviews and thirty-one four-star reviews. It had only one one-star review:

8

Foley's. Critics and industry people were calling *Anne Askew in the Tower* the next big thing. Alistair was calling to have it flushed down the commode.

He'd just finished an hour-long session with his creative writing students. He'd told them that writing was a great way of working out your feelings. He'd told them that symbolism was the most important part of any work of fiction. He'd told them they should submit their manuscripts in twelve-point Courier font, double-spaced. And he told them that they should never, ever, under any circumstances, *ever* consider self-publishing their work.

"Indie publishing is for hacks," he'd said. "No one will ever take you seriously if you go that route. It's undervaluing your art, and participating in it is joining the pitchforked multitudes in overthrowing our cultural and literary heritage."

"What about Hugh Howey?" asked a bright-eyed student in the third row.

"Whom?" said Alistair. It was a rhetorical question. Alistair had read and enjoyed Hugh Howey's work just like a million other people across the planet, but he wasn't about to admit that to his students.

"You know, he wrote *The COT-TON Omnibus*? *Hugh Howey.* Everyone's talking about him."

"Oh," said Alistair. "Him. Well, he's an exception that proves the rule."

"What about Bombo Dawson?" asked another student. "He sold his novel to a publisher in the UK, but self-published it here in the United States. Everyone is talking about him too."

Alistair leaned over his desk. His face tightened and his eyes narrowed. "Don't say that person's name in my class *ever again*, do you hear me? We discuss *literary luminaries* here—not cartoonish, donut-chomping buffoons who manage to bang out fifty thousand incoherent words on a computer between snacks. Dawson is a *hack*, do you understand me? H-A-C-K. What does that spell?"

ALISTAIR WAS STILL TREMBLING WITH rage after his students had left. He couldn't eat—just the thought of Bombo's novel made him sick—and the last thing he needed was to throw up all over the cafeteria. Especially not in the social media age. Someone would take a picture with their smartphone—maybe one of those retro-looking pictures—and post it on Facebook. And that, as they say, would be that. If he didn't get fired, he'd probably have to quit just from the shame and embarrassment of it all, and then he'd have nothing left to live for. As it was, the only thing that gave meaning to Alistair's life was literature. He spent considerable time in various realms of fantasy—since his real life basically sucked.

He lived alone in a one-bedroom apartment that was within walking distance of the community college. And his girlfriend of five years had recently dumped him like a bad habit.

"You're a great guy," Lisa had said. "Actually, that's not true. You're an asshole, and after five years I've realized that I could do better than you by literally picking any stranger off a street corner, or randomly dialing numbers until someone single picked up."

"Please," Alistair had said, "give me another chance. I can change. What do you want me to change?"

"Everything."

"Is there anything about me that you *do* like?"

Lisa thought about it. "No," she'd said. "Not that I can think of."

So, angry and feeling bitter, instead of eating lunch, Alistair decided to write a review of *Anne Askew In The Tower*. He'd read the book over the weekend, and to his disgust, couldn't get it out of his mind. He shared his review on his Twitter account, snickering to himself all the while. This is going to drive Bombo's fans crazy, he thought as he pressed the tweet button.

That was the moment—the very instant when Alistair's tweet went live—that something amazing happened. The classroom's closet door swung open, spilling a terrible light into the room. It had an otherworldly glow that gave Alistair a terrible sense of vertigo. He braced himself against his desk. *This is like something out of a fantasy novel*, he thought.

And then Thornton Wilder stepped out of the closet.

★ ★ ★

TOLSTOY HAD AN EPIC BEARD THAT PUT even Bombo's to shame. It was long and white and completely unkempt. Another man might have mistaken him for a biker, or a homeless person that had wandered into the house while Bombo and Carol were having breakfast on the terrace, but not Bombo Dawson. He recognized Tolstoy at once. Immediately he grabbed a deck chair and prepared himself to smash in his all-time-favorite author's head.

"Wait!" Tolstoy shouted. "I'm not a zombie."

"You're not?" Bombo asked. "Do you feel like eating me?"

Tolstoy scowled. "Of course not."

Bombo turned to Carol, "He's not a zombie, dear. So that's good."

"Who is this man?" Carol asked. "Do you know him?"

"It's Leo Tolstoy," Bombo said. He rolled his eyes like anybody should just know that.

"He doesn't look like a zombie," Carol said.

"I'm not," Tolstoy said. "We already covered that. I'm a ghost. There's an important difference."

"Oh yeah?" Carol said. "What could possibly be the difference? Both are dead, right? Or used to be? And both get reanimated somehow to walk around and do things and stuff?"

Tolstoy glowered at Carol. "The difference is significant, I tell you!"

Carol stared at him for a moment as the terrace began to rotate slowly all around her.

"Carol?" Bombo said. "Are you all right?"

"I don't feel so good," she said. After a few wobbly seconds, her eyes rolled back in her head and she fainted. Lucky for her, Bombo was remarkably light on his feet for a man his size. He caught her as she fell back and eased her gently to the deck.

"Your wife appears to have fainted," Tolstoy said.

"Sorry about that," Bombo said. "She's been on a vegetarian diet and we all know that avoiding meat isn't actually all that healthy."

"I'm a vegetarian," Tolstoy said. "Or, I used to be when I was alive."

"Oh," Bombo said. "I didn't realize…"

"That's fine," Tolstoy said. "Don't worry about it."

"Would you like a donut?" Bombo asked. He picked up the box and offered it to the author of *War and Peace*. Tolstoy looked over the box with great care, as if the next decision he made might affect the fate of the world. After several moments, he selected a plain glazed.

"Thank you," Tolstoy said.

"No problem," said Bombo. He looked from Tolstoy to Carol. "Maybe I should try to wake her up or something."

"Perhaps you should wait," Tolstoy said. "What I'm about to tell you might be upsetting to her."

"She survived a zombie apocalypse," Bombo said. "She's pretty tough… for a vegetarian."

"Be that as it may," Tolstoy said, "what I have to say is for your ears alone."

Bombo nodded. "Okay then, lay it on me."

"I come from a place called the Legendarium," Tolstoy said. "It is a sacred place to all writers."

"Is it a place where all the stories are collected?" Bombo asked.

"Yes," Tolstoy said. "How did you know that?"

"Lucky guess."

"There are forces at work to destroy the Legendarium…"

"And you want me to help defend it, right?"

"Yes," Tolstoy said. "And how did you know that?"

"Hugh Howey called me about twenty minutes ago," Bombo said. "He told me this crazy story about Kurt Vonnegut and this metaphysical library. I thought he was playing a practical joke or trying to lure me down to Florida so he could eat my brain."

"I can assure you," Tolstoy said, "this is no joke."

"Well," Bombo said," I suppose I've got nothing better to do. What about Carol?"

"She'll be fine," Tolstoy said. "You can tend to her when you get back."

Bombo looked from Carol to Tolstoy. He looked from Tolstoy to Carol. He looked at the donuts. He took one with zebra-striped frosting. "Okay," he said and took a bite. "Let's do this!"

As he spoke, donut crumbs sprayed out of his mouth, and a few caught in Tolstoy's beard. Bombo reached over to the Russian's beard and began trying to pick out the crumbs but as he did, sugar clumps that had been stuck to his fingers replaced the crumbs he was trying to remove. Overall, as he worked in silence, the problem of donut shrapnel in Tolstoy's beard got worse and worse. After an awkward thirty seconds or so of the author of *War and Peace* glaring at him, the great writer finally smacked Bombo's hand and pointed toward the glowing door.

Bombo stepped over Carol and followed Leo Tolstoy through the door—and into the glowing light of the Legendarium.

THE DISTANCE FROM THE SURFACE OF Alistair Foley's desk to the floor seemed to wobble and stretch as the creative writing teacher attempted to rise. He lurched forward and nearly fell, but managed to keep his feet.

"Are you quite all right?" Thornton Wilder's voice rose in the middle of every sentence and tapered off at the end. His hair was cut so short that he was almost bald. He wore round, Harry-Potter-type glasses and had a neatly trimmed mustache.

"I—I think so," said Alistair.

"My name is Thornton Wilder," Thornton Wilder said. "Are you Alistair Foley?"

"I, um… yes." Alistair shook his head, trying to make sense of what was happening.

"I'm going to say some things that might upset you," said Thornton Wilder. "They might hurt your feelings if you're particularly set in your mind about scientific laws and the structure of the universe. But what I have to say is important, and—"

"How can you be here?" Alistair said. "You died almost forty years ago." He staggered, and would have fallen if Wilder hadn't caught him at the last minute. The Pulitzer Prize-winning author helped the creative writing teacher back to his seat.

"I need you to listen," said Thornton Wilder. "This world isn't all that there is. There are thousands—"

"Are you one of those zombies they had over in London last year? The ones that only ate good writers?"

Thornton Wilder sighed as he leaned against Foley's desk. He shifted his Harry Potter glasses on his nose. "If I were, I imagine you'd be perfectly safe. But I'm not."

Alistair winced. "Ouch."

I'll try to explain," he said. "It's like this: when a writer dies, a part of their spirit lives on in a place called the Legendarium."

"Like Tolkien's Legendarium?"

"No," Wilder said. "Well, sort of. That was pure fiction. This Legendarium is a real library, a repository of every story ever told. It touches every world—"

"Every… world?"

"There are thousands, millions of other worlds out there," Wilder said. "One for each novel or short story ever published. Some scientists might call it a multiverse, and that's as good a name as any. Of the other worlds, many are just like this one, only with subtle differences. In some, the South won the Civil War. In others, the North won, but perhaps Abraham Lincoln was never assassinated. Do you follow me so far?"

"Like alternative histories?" Alistair said.

Wilder nodded. "Yes, but in the Legendarium the history of those stories is not *alternative*. It is the real world created by that author. And although the writer's words do not directly affect what happens or exists in this world, they do affect the readers of those words that live in this world. In that way, the relationship between worlds is very, very real."

Alistair rubbed his eyes and then scratched his head. "Okay, if those worlds are real to the people in them, then how do I know that I'm not the character in someone else's story? How do I know that I'm real?"

Wilder smiled, and when he did, his glasses slipped a few centimeters down his nose so that he was looking over them at Alistair. "I'll answer your question with a question, sir. In what fictional world would any writer worth their salt allow *you* to teach people about writing? All you have is a degree; you've never actually published!"

Alistair scowled. "That hurts… just a little bit."

"My apologies, sir," Wilder said. "But I wanted to keep you on point. We have no time for digressions. So, do you understand what I've told you so far?"

"I think so," Alistair said. In truth, he was beginning to think that he was suffering a schizophrenic episode. This was not entirely out of the range of possibility. Alistair's great-grandfather had suffered from schizophrenia, and it was a very real possibility that any male descendant of that great-grandfather could one day be rendered a lunatic, unable to distinguish reality from fantasy. Still, Thornton Wilder had a point about Alistair being allowed to teach creative writing at the college level. He hoped to be a great writer one day, but he was hardly an expert. That alone gave some credence to the idea that perhaps what was happening was actually real.

"There are yet other worlds," Thornton Wilder was saying, "where human beings live alongside elves and other creatures, and dragons are real. I don't mean to go on and on, but I want you to understand that all of these worlds exist within the mind of God. They exist, and in every single one there is a place where it overlaps all the others. We call that overlapping place the Legendarium."

"I don't understand any of this," Alistair said. "Maybe I have food poisoning. Am I going to be visited by three ghosts?"

"Of course not," Wilder snapped. "Don't be ridiculous. This isn't that world."

"I'm hallucinating."

"I can assure you," Thornton Wilder said, "that you are not."

"But you're dead. And you appeared out of the broom closet. And you're Thornton Wilder."

"Jesus wept. Listen to me," Thornton Wilder said. "The Legendarium is very real—and it is in trouble. Something is corrupting the multiverse, and if it isn't put to a stop, all human knowledge will be wiped out. Do you understand that? If you don't help me, the world is going to slip back into the dark ages, or worse."

Alistair stared at him without comprehension. Food poisoning would be easier to deal with than schizophrenia, and it would explain the way his stomach lurched when Thornton Wilder walked into the room. On the other hand, Wilder seemed quite real and the nausea was now gone.

"I need you to come with me," said Thornton Wilder. "I've been sent to recruit you. Will you help me?"

Foley sighed. Whatever the cause of this hallucination, it wasn't going away. Perhaps he had to let it play out to the end, and then everything would return to normal. "I have another class in twenty minutes. Is this going to take a long time?"

Thornton Wilder adjusted his glasses again. "Time has no meaning in the Legendarium," he said. "When you return, *if* you return, it will be at the exact moment that you left."

"Well, that's convenient," Alistair said.

"Will you go then?" Wilder asked. "Will you defend the Legendarium?"

Alistair Foley's eyes scanned his classroom. He thought about all the books he'd read where this kind of thing happened. He thought about all of the one-star reviews he'd given those books on his blog. "Might as well," he said at last. "Do I need to bring anything?"

"Your wits," said Thornton Wilder. "You're going to need them."

The Pulitzer Prize-winning author of *Our Town* extended his hand, and Alistair Foley took it. He rose and followed the great writer to the broom closet. It excited Alistair more than a little to hope that somewhere—some*when*—he'd be coming out of the closet with Thornton Wilder into a whole new reality.

Wilder turned the doorknob and opened the door. A terrible white light spilled into the room, but this time Alistair was expecting it and he felt fine. Wilder stepped through the doorway and into the light. A moment later, Alistair Foley followed him into the Legendarium.

CHAPTER TWO:
THROUGH THE LOOKING GLASS AND INTO THE FIRE

THE FIRST THING THAT HIT BOMBO Dawson as he entered the Legendarium was the smell. It was musty and leathery and sweet and acrid all at the same time. It was the smell of eternity and ink and the distilled creative labors of lifetimes.

It took a moment for his eyes to adjust, and when they did, Bombo saw that he was standing in a circular room filled with books from floor to ceiling. Maybe it wasn't a circle, he thought. Maybe it was an octagon, or an oblong cylinder. He'd forgotten everything he'd ever learned in geometry class, but it certainly seemed circular-ish. Or maybe it was oval-ish. Anyway, there was one half of a French door behind him—and it looked exactly like the door that led to his terrace.

"Wow," Bombo said as he stared at the painted domed ceiling overhead. A fresco painted on the underside of the dome portrayed the Battle of Helm's Deep from *The Lord of the Rings.*

"Beautiful, isn't it?" Tolstoy said. "And this is just the parlor."

Bombo wiped a tear from his eye. "The fresco… I don't like fantasy much, but it's amazing."

"Leonardo da Vinci painted it," Tolstoy said.

"You're joking," Bombo said. "He died something like four hundred years before Tolkien was born."

"Time has no meaning in the Legendarium," Tolstoy said.

"I thought you said we were in a hurry," Bombo said.

Tolstoy glared at Bombo. "Even in timelessness things happen in order."

Bombo winced, sheepishly. "Well, you see… the word 'order' implies—"

"Quit being insolent, fat man," Tolstoy interrupted. "I don't have time to explain it all to you."

"You see, there you said—"

"SILENCE!" Tolstoy shouted. "I know what I said! I am a committed pacifist, Mr. Dawson. Please do not try my patience any further!"

"All right, then," Bombo said. "Proceed." After he said "proceed," though, he giggled to himself.

Leo Tolstoy glared at Bombo Dawson, but said nothing.

Bombo finally stopped giggling when he saw that Tolstoy was truly irritated with him. "You see… sir… even the word 'proceed' has a time element to it."

"Are you quite finished?" Tolstoy said.

"Yes," Bombo said. "But… again… the word 'finished'…"

Tolstoy went back to glaring at Bombo, which cut the chubby author short again.

"I'm sorry, sir," Bombo said. "All done." A muted giggle erupted from the large man, but this time he successfully silenced it.

Tolstoy waited for a half minute (which had no meaning in the Legendarium) to make sure Bombo was indeed finished before he continued. "Now, if you will please follow me, we have to get down to business."

They crossed the large chamber, and the brisk pace winded Bombo. He realized that he was beginning to regret that last donut. *Maybe Carol is right*, he thought. *Maybe I should go on a diet.* The thought filled him with profound sorrow, but he didn't have time to ponder if for long. On the far side of the room was an archway that led into an enormous room. The ceiling seemed to stretch up forever, and on every story were landings filled from floor to ceiling with books.

"Wow," Bombo said. "This place is just… wow."

"You should see the Russian room over in the east wing," Tolstoy said. "Breathtaking. I'll have to show it to once you've completed your mission." He paused, cleared his throat, and then added in a whisper, "Assuming you make it back alive."

"I was wondering something," Bombo said.

"What's that?"

"What about Vonnegut?" Bombo said. "Hugh Howey told me that he was visited by Kurt Vonnegut. Why did they send you instead of him?"

Tolstoy looked embarrassed, but quickly recovered. "To tell you the truth," he said, "I wanted to meet you. I really enjoyed *Anne Askew in the Tower*."

"Really?" Bombo said. "Thanks."

"Of course," Tolstoy said, "I didn't realize you could be such an insufferable clown in person."

"I have my serious times," Bombo said.

"Let's hope you do, young man."

As they spoke, they heard footsteps approaching in the distance. They turned in the direction of the footsteps and saw a white-robed figure that appeared to be Thornton Wilder. At his side was a middle-aged man in a threadbare professor's jacket.

"Leo," Wilder said. "It's good to see you."

"And you," Tolstoy said. The ghostly writers shook hands. Tolstoy gestured toward Bombo. "I want you to meet—"

"Bombo Dawson!" said Alistair Foley. "You've got to be kidding me."

"Excuse me?" said Thornton Wilder.

"What is he going on about?" said Leo Tolstoy.

"Do you know me?" Bombo asked. "I don't think I know you. Nice ponytail, by the way, ma'am."

"I am a *man*, and I know all about *you*," Alistair spat. "I just reviewed your stupid little novel. It was terrible. Terrible!"

Tolstoy straightened. "If you are speaking of *Anne Askew in the Tower*, I must strenuously disagree, sir!" The great Russian author put his hands behind his back and stuck out his chest. "I read Mr. Dawson's book, and I found it to be quite good."

Alistair sneered. "Well, what would you know? It took you almost two hundred pages to describe a dinner party!"

Tolstoy's anger flared again and he took a step toward Alistair, but Bombo stepped forward first, his face reddened with fury. "You," he said. "You're the jerk that wrote that one-star review."

"I would be that jerk," said Alistair.

"Gentlemen," said Thornton Wilder. "Please, we need to brief you on your mission. The fate of the world is at stake."

"You didn't tell me that I would be working with *this* idiot," Alistair said. "Now I *know* that this is a hallucination, because there's no chance that Bombo Dawson—of all people!—would be chosen to defend this *so-called* Legendarium."

"And what makes *you* qualified for this mission?" Bombo asked. "I've had one hundred and nineteen reviews of my novel, and one hundred and eighteen of them are four-star or better."

Alistair started to answer, but he stopped himself. He turned to Thornton Wilder. "That's actually a good question," he said. "Why would you choose me? I've never published anything."

Wilder and Tolstoy exchanged a look.

"You've never *published* anything," Wilder said, "but you have *written* something."

Alistair's eyes widened. "How do you know that?" he demanded.

"I've read it," said the man who'd won not one but *two* Pulitzer Prizes (most people don't know that). "The finished version, that is."

"Me too," said Tolstoy. "It still needs some revision in the now, but the future final version… it's good."

"Was it written in crayon?" Bombo said, laughing at his own jab.

"You're one to talk," Alistair snapped. "At least I had the good sense not to publish before I was ready. Ever heard of an editor?"

"Have you ever heard of a wannabe that criticizes people because they've done something that he can't?" Bombo took a threatening step toward Alistair. He stood at least six inches taller than the creative writing teacher, and outweighed him by well over a hundred pounds (though this might have been cut to sixty or seventy pounds if Bombo had adhered to Carol's dieting advice).

Tolstoy, the father of Christian anarchism and a profound pacifist, shoved himself between the new author and his harshest critic. "You must stop this," he said. "There are larger things at stake than your foolish egos."

"A minute ago you wanted to pound him, Leo," Bombo said, glaring at Alistair.

"I'll admit he is… a frustrating man," Tolstoy said. "But let's not lose our heads."

"You two are going to have to learn to work together," said Wilder, "or the multiverse is doomed. Worlds are dying while you two stand around arguing."

Bombo and Alistair stared into each other's eyes like two professional wrestlers about to embark on the match of their career. The tension was palpable.

"I can never work with this idiot," Alistair said. His voice was slow and steady.

"Well now," Bombo said. "Something on which we can both agree!" His eyes cut upward as he tried to recall exactly what he was claiming to agree with. "Well… except the part about me being an idiot. We completely *dis*agree on that part. *He's* the idiot. And he has a ponytail."

Wilder and Tolstoy exchanged an exasperated look. There was nothing either ghost writer could say that would make an impression on Bombo Dawson or Alistair Foley. The two ghosts' eyes met and they both nodded. This was no time for words; it was a time for action.

Tolstoy moved casually behind the living authors as they continued their argument. Wilder, meanwhile, knelt down and pulled on a heavy iron ring in the floor. A trap door opened, and white light spilled into the room. Tolstoy reached out with both hands and shoved both Bombo and Alistair toward the opening. They teetered for a moment on the edge of the light, their arms waving in a futile effort to regain their balance, and then they were falling…

Falling…

Falling…

THEY LANDED WITH A SPLASH.

Alistair Foley, who maintained a membership at a local health club and swam twice weekly, bobbed right to the surface. *Well, apparently gravity isn't meaningless in the Legendarium,* he thought. He spit out a mouthful of salty water and tried to get his bearings. He was in a pond in the midst of a sylvan wood. Birds sang in the distance, and he could smell the slightest aroma of sulfur in the air.

There was a sound like someone sobbing, but looking around, Alistair couldn't see anyone. It was at that moment that something brushed against him. It took him a moment to recognize that it was a flannel shirt.

Bombo's shirt. Empty. Meaning that there wasn't an overweight, bearded writer in it.

"Dawson?" Alistair shouted. "Where are you?"

There was no response.

"Stupid fat moron," Alistair whispered. "Of all the terrible hallucinations, I'm stuck—"

Something grabbed Alistair's ankle. He screamed and kicked his feet, knocking whatever it was away. He looked down into the abyss, and saw a terrible sight: Bombo Dawson was on the bottom of the pond, his face contorted in fear, and his hands reaching toward Alistair in desperation.

Instinctively, Alistair took in a huge gulp of air and dove. The saltiness stung his eyes, but he kicked downward anyway. He touched the bottom of the pond, grabbed Bombo by the collar, and pushed off. They rose together steadily, Alistair kicking his feet all the way, and a moment later breached the surface of the water.

The creative writing teacher took a huge gulp of air. He was alive, but he wasn't sure he could say the same thing about Bombo. With one arm over the shoulder and across the chest of his mortal enemy, Foley lay back in the water and began paddling toward the shore. In this way, he kept Bombo's head above water, though the man was unconscious, and his large head lolled from side to side with each stroke. It felt like an eternity, but within a minute they were on the bank of the small pond. With much effort Alistair dragged Bombo out of the water and checked for signs of life.

Bombo wasn't breathing.

Alistair turned Bombo's head to the side, allowing the water in his mouth and nose to drain away. Next, he turned the bearded man's head forward and prepared to give him mouth-to-mouth.

It was at that moment that Bombo's eyes popped open. He saw Alistair hovering over him, lips pursed and just beginning to open.

"No!" Bombo shouted. He gagged and coughed. "Don't do it!" He squirmed to the side, narrowly avoiding an uncomfortably intimate moment with his most hated rival.

"Oh, thank God," Alistair said. He rolled off of Bombo and pushed himself to his feet.

The two writers scurried away from one another, both avoiding eye contact as if it might reinitiate the terrible scenario they'd just endured. An uncomfortable silence descended on the two, the only sound that of someone weeping in the distance.

"Um, thanks," Bombo said. He halfway stuck his hand out like he wanted to shake, but midway through the gesture he stopped and just kind of awkwardly waved at Alistair. "You saved my life."

"Don't mention it," Alistair said. "I would have done it for anyone." He put his hands on his hips and then looked around. "Except for that Tolstoy. I could kill him for pushing us down that hole."

Bombo shrugged and then bent over with his hands on his knees to catch his breath. "He's already dead."

Alistair gave Bombo a nasty look. "I was speaking metaphorically."

"No," Bombo said, "you were speaking *ironically*, only even *you* didn't know it." He inhaled deeply and then stood up again and nodded his head at Alistair. "What you meant to do is use *hyperbole*. I can't believe they let you teach young people."

"Why didn't I just let you die?" Alistair said.

"Now *that*," Bombo said, "was meant to be rhetorical, I suppose."

Alistair glared at Bombo and his hands clenched into fists.

"I never learned how to swim," explained Bombo.

"You never learned how to write either," said Alistair.

Bombo started to go on the attack again, but then changed his mind. He would allow the snide remark to pass, at least this once. He owed Alistair Foley his life; not responding to his obnoxious trolling for five minutes was the least he could do.

Over in the pond, Bombo watched as his flannel shirt drifted lazily toward shore. The weeping in the distance went on and on.

"What's that sound?" Bombo asked.

Alistair listened for a moment. "It sounds like somebody crying."

"Do you have any idea what story this is?" said Bombo as he reached into the pond and retrieved his shirt.

"None," Foley said. "This little piece of forest could be virtually any scene in almost any book, a fairy tale, a fantasy novel… anything."

"I hate fantasy," Bombo said. "Most fantasy novels are so lame."

"I love fantasy," Alistair said, "but I know what you mean. So many are just cheap knockoffs of—" he stopped, realizing that he had just agreed with Bombo on a point concerning literature. He wondered if somewhere, in another part of the Legendarium, Hell was freezing over. But he didn't have to worry. His agreement with Bombo didn't last long.

"I mean, what's the deal?" Bombo said. "It's like a bunch of pre-teens sitting around a campfire making up a story on the fly." He adopted the voice of a young boy. "Okay, a guy named Bob was going to Cleveland to sign some insurance papers." Then Bombo imitated the voice of a young girl. "No, no, no… His name isn't Bob, it's Bogrith the Vendarme." Bombo was now hopping back and forth between the two characters, acting out his scene. In the boy's voice: "Okay, so Bogrith the Vendarme is going to Cleveland to sign some insurance papers… No wait! He's not going to Cleveland. He's going to the ancient city of Chlamydia!" Now Bombo hopped over to the girl's place and put on her voice: "Yes! And Bogrith the Vendarme is going to Chlamydia to rescue the Oracle of Boobstone!"

"Stop it," Alistair said.

"Oh, and there were elves and dwarves and stuff," Bombo added in his childish voice.

"Just stop it," Alistair repeated. "You are a complete nit." The sound of the person crying in the distance caught his attention again, but he couldn't leave off without trying to knock some sense into Bombo. "Just because *most* fantasy stories are nonsense doesn't mean that fantasy isn't a valid form of literature. When it's done well, it can be very good."

Bombo laughed, but his his laugh dripped with sarcasm and derision. "It sucks because it isn't *real*."

"All fiction is unreal at some level," Alistair added. He was now staring into the middle distance with a philosophical look on his face. "Maybe that's why we need to save the Legendarium. Because at another level, all fiction is *very* real."

Bombo pulled on his flannel shirt and buttoned the top few buttons. "I guess."

"As much as this pains me," Alistair said, "it appears that we're going to have to work together if we have any hope of returning to our normal lives."

"Yes," Bombo said. "I have to return to a world where I'm a bestselling author, and you have to return to a world where that ponytail is okay. So… any idea where we go from here? I don't see a yellow brick road."

"We should track around and see if we can find the source of the crying," Alistair said, deciding not to take the bait on the ponytail comment. "That seems like the logical thing to do here."

Bombo thought about it for a minute. "Agreed. Let's do this."

The soggy writers walked along the perimeter of the pond, their wet socks squishing with every step. Soon they came to a tiny stream that led into the woods. The sound of the weeping seemed louder in that direction, so they agreed to follow the stream and see where it led.

"Hopefully whoever is up there crying is doing it next to a warm fire," Alistair said.

"Hopefully they have some marshmallows and chocolate and graham crackers," Bombo said. "I could go for some s'mores."

As they walked, Bombo mimed making a s'more. First he held an imaginary coat hanger with a marshmallow on it over a fire. Then he pulled back the marshmallow and blew on it to cool it. He touched it with his fingers and pulled them back and shook his hand to show his companion how hot it was. He looked over at Alistair, who was staring at him with a look of contempt on his face. Bombo pulled off the marshmallow and put it on an imaginary graham cracker, covered it with an imaginary chunk of chocolate, placed the graham cracker that went on top, and then sank his teeth into his invisible snack. When he was done, he sighed.

"I would love a s'more right now," he said.

"I'd like this dream a lot better if you would shut up," Alistair said.

"Or hot dogs," said Bombo. "I really like hot dogs."

THEY REACHED THE SOURCE OF THE stream after thirty minutes of hiking. The sun was now shining brightly and the heat was inundating the forest. Bombo was breathing heavily, but his clothes were nearly dry, except for the areas where his sweat had kept the clothing damp.

Alistair wasn't even winded. After all, he was in good shape, thanks to his gym membership—it wasn't like he had anything else to do after work.

"Has anyone ever told you that you smell funny?" Alistair asked. "You just took a salty bath and already you reek."

Bombo shrugged. "It might have been mentioned before. I don't really recall," he said. "I prefer to think of myself as being *odiferous*."

"You smell like broccoli," Alistair said.

"Now that's just hurtful."

"Or maybe asparagus."

"That's more like it," Bombo said with a smile.

The sound of someone crying increased with every step, and finally the two writers saw a man in silver armor leaning against a tree in a small clearing in the woods.

"It's Don Quixote!" Bombo said. "The ingenious gentleman knight himself!"

Alistair shook his head. "No it isn't."

"It is!" Bombo said. "And we're in La Mancha! So sweet! I love this story!"

"We're not in La Mancha, you dolt," Alistair said. "Look at his ridiculous mustaches. A blond mustache that completely covers his mouth. Quixote was a Spaniard, and they didn't usually wear mustaches like that. And certainly not a blond one covering his mouth. Cervantes would have said something about it if the man looked that way."

Bombo leaned forward to stare at the knight. "But…"

"But nothing," Alistair said. "And where is Sancho Panza? Do you see Sancho Panza?"

"Well… no."

"This is another story, then," Alistair proclaimed, triumphantly.

The weeping knight did indeed have ridiculous blonde mustaches that completely covered his mouth. And the man seemed to be not only the source the weeping, but of the stream as well. His tears fell down his face and ran downhill toward the pond. Bombo and Alistair followed the stream with their eyes, and then they looked at one another. It seemed that the pond they'd landed in was actually the collected tears of this one anguished knight.

"Sirs," said the weeping knight, "I wonder if the both of you hast seen a sword during your travels?"

"No, sir," Bombo said.

"We haven't seen anything," said Alistair.

"Beware the Jabberwocky, my son!" said the knight. "So spake my lord as I departed the castle. The jaws that bite, the claws that catch! How shall I battle the fiend without my sword?"

Bombo and Alistair shared another look.

"*Now* do you recognize this story?" Bombo asked.

"*Alice in Wonderland*," Alistair said. "Or is it *Through The Looking Glass*?"

"*Looking Glass*," said Bombo. "I wonder if the books share a world, or if each one has its own door."

"If I recall correctly," Alistair said, "the knight in Lewis Carroll's poem defeated the Jabberwocky with the vorpal blade. Perhaps if he doesn't have it…"

"Then the Jabberwocky might play a different role in the story. It could hinder Alice…"

"Or kill her or otherwise change the ending of the story."

"The vorpal blade went snicker-snack," Bombo said.

"Yes!" said the knight. "That's my sword. Have you seen it?" There was desperation in his eyes.

"We haven't," Bombo said, "but we'd be happy to help you look for it."

"When did you see it last?" Alistair asked.

The knight thought about it. "I broke for camp upon this spot last eve," he said. "The vorpal sword 'twas by my side where I keep it always. When I awoke upon the morn, it was gone."

"Someone stole it in the night," Bombo said. He rubbed his chin and nodded his head like he'd come to some fantastic conclusion.

"'Tis true," said the knight. "And without it, the Jabberwocky's reign of destruction will continue unhindered."

"How in the world are we going to find his sword?" Alistair said. "Which way do we go?"

"That depends a good deal on where you want to get to," said a smug voice.

Bombo and Alistair looked up into the trees, where they saw a disembodied grin hovering in the branches overhead. A striped cat—the Cheshire Cat—began to materialize behind the smile.

"I guess this answers the question of whether this story shares the same world as *Alice in Wonderland*," Bombo said.

"When I get home I'm going to review both of these books," Alistair said. "Have I ever mentioned that I hate Lewis Carroll?"

"Well, I see I'm in good company," Bombo said. "You hate Bombo Dawson, Leo Tolstoy, and Lewis Carroll."

"I don't hate Tolstoy," Alistair said. "I was just irritated."

Bombo nodded. "But you hate me and Lewis Carroll?"

"Deeply," Alistair said, nodding.

"But *Wonderland* is fantasy—and you love fantasy."

"Wonderland is just nonsense. Are you saying that you like it?"

"Yep."

"But you hate fantasy," Alistair smiled triumphantly, as if he'd just caught Bombo in a trap.

"My mom read it to me when I was a boy," Bombo said. "I've had a soft spot for Lewis Carroll ever since."

"You like a fantasy novel."

"So shoot me," said Bombo. "At least there aren't any elves."

"I saw who took his sword," interrupted the Cheshire Cat. "Or is it whom? Who… whom… who… whom… I can never remember."

"Who," said Bombo.

"Whom," said Alistair.

"There was a Jubjub bird," said the cat. "A black bird. A raven. Or maybe it was a rook. It was quite large."

"It took the sword?" Alistair asked.

"Who did?" said the cat.

"The raven," Alistair said.

"The rook," said the cat. "The rook took the sword."

"Did you see which way he went?" Bombo asked.

"Who said she was a he?" asked the cat.

"Did you see which way she went?" said Alistair.

"That way," said the cat. Its tail writhed this way and that, and then pointed toward the west. "Say, have you tried the borogoves? They're delicious."

"Please," the knight wept, "you must find my sword."

"Come on," Bombo said. "The sooner we get this over with, the sooner we can get home."

"Hopefully," Alistair said. "Because this awful dream is getting old. This wouldn't be so bad if you were a beautiful woman instead of the worst writer I've ever read."

"Did you say something?" Bombo asked. "I couldn't hear you with your head stuck so impertinently up your own ass."

They headed north through the *tulgey* wood, and the *slithy toves gyred* and *gimbled* in the *wabe*. They seldom spoke as they walked, preferring silence to each other's company. Alistair was writing a review in his head for the beloved works of Lewis Carroll. The review was scathing. He was hoping to use the word "syphilitic" somewhere in his review, but he hadn't quite gotten the words right just yet. *You can't stick "syphilitic" just anywhere in the text—not without really thinking about it and making it just right,* he thought.

For his part, Bombo thought of donuts as he walked. Donuts made the world a better place. Blueberry cake donuts were his favorite. One day his new wife asked him why he liked blueberry cake donuts. He'd just looked at her and said, very slowly, "Blueberry. Cake. Donuts. Right there in the name are three things I like about 'em." She'd replied with, "Well, I like blueberry muffins." His response had been, "Okay, so take that delicious muffin, deep-fry it in grease, then coat it with sugar, and you got yourself paradise, m'lady." Yep. He could use a blueberry cake donut right about now. And a cigar would certainly improve the situation. The one he'd had in his shirt pocket had been ruined by his plunge into the knight's lachrymal pond, and unless he came upon a hookah-smoking caterpillar, his chances of a good smoke in this world were highly unlikely.

"Now, I'm just asking this out of curiosity," Alistair said as they walked. "But what do we care if a few stories here and there blink out of existence?"

Bombo thought about the question for a moment before answering. "The way Tolstoy explained it to me," he said, "was that every story affects someone, even if it is only the original author. And those effects change history at some level. Every one of them. I know that when I was young boy, I was profoundly affected by a book called *A Squirrel Forever,* by Douglas Fairbairn. It was a book I checked out of the public library when I was ten or so. Not many people ever read that book, and almost no one remembers it today, but I read it, and it affected me so much that it made me want to write my own stories."

"I get that," Alistair said. "The book *Rascal,* by Sterling North, had the same effect on me."

"On the other hand," Bombo continued, "another book I read at that time was the non-fiction story of *Kon-Tiki* by Thor Heyerdahl. A lot of people read that true story about men sailing across the Pacific Ocean on a raft, and its effect was far more universal. Some of the original Apollo astronauts credited reading *Kon-Tiki* with motivating them to become explorers. If those books hadn't been written, then I'd be a different person today, and the results would cascade outward for good or for evil. One way or the other, the whole world would be a different place."

Bombo and Alistair lapsed into silence as they continued through the forest. And the farther they walked, the more they noticed a strange sort of feeling creeping over them. There was something in the woods watching them. They were not alone.

"Foley," Bombo said, "do you feel that?"

"The feeling that the shadows between the trees are alive and hostile?" said Alistair, "or the feeling of utter revulsion that washes over me when you call me by my last name."

"That first thing you said," Bombo said. "The one about the shadows being hostile."

The temperature dropped drastically, and if Bombo had been a beautiful woman, Alistair would have gladly snuggled up to her. But he wasn't, so the creative writing teacher simply stood there, shivering, as the shadows in the woods began to move.

★ ★ ★

THEY WERE CALLED THE *MOME WRAITHS*, creatures of living shadow that dwelt in the space between worlds. They were an ancient race, and some say that they were the fallen angels of lore. They had no knowledge of peace or joy, no understanding of love. Theirs was a life of emptiness and hatred and ignorance. They saw light in men's eyes and they wanted to extinguish it.

The Mome Wraiths were born of the void in which the world was made. They were the darkness on the face of the deep. They were present at the foundation of life on earth, and they would never rest until all knowledge was wiped out and the world was returned once more to shadow and chaotic emptiness.

The Mome Wraiths watched as two beyonders passed through the Tulgey Wood. They watched, and their black hearts burned with hatred. These squabbling heroes had the power to unravel the darkness and save the worlds from destruction. The Mome Wraiths would not let that happen.

As the beyonders passed by, the Mome Wraiths poured from the trees like oil spilling from an undersea well. They seeped toward our heroes, moaning and shrieking and stretching forth their clawed hands. One touch was all it would take. One touch would suck out a living creature's soul and turn that creature into a Mome Wraith.

"Run!" shouted the largest beyonder. He shoved his companion toward a narrow opening between the Mome Wraiths, and the Mome Wraiths moved quickly to close the gap. In a few seconds, these heroes would become living shadows, and the last hope for the world would slip into darkness.

★ ★ ★

"RUN!" BOMBO SHOUTED. HE SHOVED Alistair, and the smaller man nearly stumbled. Bombo grabbed him by the shirt at the last possible second and helped his arch-nemesis to regain his balance. Bombo was surprisingly nimble for such a large man, especially when he felt like he was in danger.

Together they ran, narrowly slipping past the encompassing shadows before the Mome Wraiths closed their circle. The trees sped past—or, in Bombo's case, lumbered past, —but both of our heroes understood that it was only a matter of time before their luck would run out. The woods were teeming with the living shadows, and there was nowhere to go.

Still they ran and ran. Alistair's lungs were burning, and Bombo was certain he was about to die. His thoughts flashed, for just a moment, to the time that he'd run through the streets of London with Hugh Howey—being chased by zombies. He remembered how he'd admitted to himself at that moment that he probably needed to get into better shape. Human minds often thrash around in moments of peril, he thought, and promise things here and there like offerings at the altar of some covetous deity. That's probably what all that nonsense was around New Year's Day—the resolutions and so forth. But now, the desire to amend his ways *seemed* very real. These weren't some slowpoke zombified writers he was running from. These things were *spiritual*. They gave off the odor of actual *evil*, embodied in shadow form, only with scary claws and other assorted devilish whatnots.

If only I'd listened to Carol, he thought. He wondered if she was still lying on their deck, unconscious. *Of course she is*, he thought. The ghost writers had told him that time was meaningless in the

Legendarium. Bombo shook his head. It seemed like hours since they'd told him that, but it was probably only minutes ago. He wondered what Carol would think if he died here. If when she awoke he was just gone and never came back.

They entered a small clearing, and for a moment it looked as if they might have outrun the immediate danger. They paused to catch their breath, their eyes searching the tree line for the onrushing evil.

"What are we going to do?" Alistair said through labored inhalations.

"I… don't…" Bombo struggled for a breath. "I… don't…" His face was slowly regaining a bit of color. "I… don't… know," he panted.

"I know," said a familiar voice.

The Cheshire Cat faded in to opacity on the ground at Bombo's feet. His eyes twinkled playfully, as if nothing out of the ordinary was happening.

"Tell us quickly, cat," Alistair said. "How do we fight those creatures?"

"What creatures?"

"Those shadows," Bombo said. "They tried to kill us back there."

"They are called the Mome Wraiths," said the cat. "But, they weren't trying to kill you."

"Ummm… I'm pretty sure they were trying to kill us," Bombo said, "Or at least it sure did seem like it to me," he added.

"If a Mome Wraith touched you," said the cat, "you would become one of them." He gave a perfect imitation of a Mome Wraith's terrible moan.

"How can we fight them?" Alistair demanded.

"You can't fight them," said the cat. "You have to find the vorpal sword."

"Can the vorpal sword hurt them?" asked Bombo.

"The vorpal sword can kill the Jabberwocky," said the cat, as if this were something that everyone should know without asking.

Bombo and Alistair looked at one another in exasperation.

"You're saying that we should keep looking for the sword?" Alistair said.

"Try the door," said the cat. He pointed once again with his tail and then began to fade.

Bombo and Alistair turned and saw something peculiar, if anything in Wonderland can be called more peculiar than any other. A metal door like something on the starship *Enterprise* was standing just a few yards off the path.

"Where do you suppose that goes?" Bombo asked.

Alistair shrugged. "Anywhere is better than here."

"But we haven't found the sword."

"Maybe the rook took it through the door," said Alistair.

There was a ghastly rumble and the sound of approaching dread, and the two authors turned and looked over their shoulders. Behind them, the Mome Wraiths were writhing and boiling through the trees, their moans growing more ominous with every second.

Bombo grabbed Alistair by the elbow and pulled him forward. "Let's go, Foley."

As they rushed toward the door, it slid open with a *swish*. White light poured from the opening, obliterating any view of what was on the other side. The Mome Wraiths were only inches away when Bombo and Alistair leapt through the portal and the door swished closed behind them.

TO BE CONTINUED IN LITERARY OUTLAW #6

WRITTEN BY **MARVIN WOLFMAN**

ILLUSTRATED BY **DON HECK** AND **MIKE ESPOSITO**

THERE, BRANDON THE BLACKSMITH. A RHYME FOR HIM!
AWAY! I HAVE NO TIME FOR SUCH FOOLISHNESS!
BRANDON THEN IT SHALL BE A SONG WITH LI-GHT TOMFOOLERY.
THERE STANDS MIGHTY BRANDON, IRONCLAD, WITH MUSCLES STRONG AND TEMPER BAD. HE HAS NO TIME FOR THIS DITTY, FOR HIS MIND IS SMALL, OH SAD PITY.
I DON'T LIKE YOUR SONG, SINGER. TAKE IT BACK OR I'LL CRUSH YOU!
I HAD NO WISH TO OFFEND YOU!
IF YOU WISH AN APOLOGY, THEN LISTEN THUS...
NO, MINSTREL. YOU SHALL NOT APOLOGIZE!
ALL EYES TURN TOWARDS THE HARSH VOICE, AND THEY SEE...
CASSANDRA... QUEEN OF THE SEVENTH WIND!
THIS IS NO BUSINESS OF YOURS, WITCH. BE OFF!
SOME SAY SHE IS A GODDESS COME FROM HEAVEN...
SILENCE, BRUTISH OAF. MINSTREL, APOLOGIZE NOT. YOUR RHYME RINGS TRUE.
WHILE OTHERS INSIST SHE IS BUT A WITCH TO BE BURNED AT HELL'S STAKE!
I SAID AWAY. A WOMAN HAS NO PLACE HERE.
YOU WHO THINK WITH YOUR MUSCLES INSTEAD INSTEAD OF YOUR HEAD ALWAYS BELIEVE A WOMAN TO BE INFERIOR.
MUST LEARN, OAF!
YAGGHHH!
WHAT ARE YOU DOING... WHAA??
DEMONSTRATING MY INFERIORITY, FOOL.
HIGHER AND HIGHER INTO THE FERVID SKIES BRANDON GOES, UNTIL...
I TIRE OF THIS BOORISH EXHIBITION. DOWN, BRANDON...DOWN TO THE GROUND.
I LIKE YOU, MINSTREL. WOULD YOU CARE TO JOIN DAMON AND MYSELF IN OUR QUEST? I OFFER NO REWARD, LEST YOU ENJOY ENDLESS ADVENTURE.
I WOULD FIND IT AN HONOR, LOVELY CASSANDRA.

BUT THE GAIETY THAT IS CALADAN IS NOWHERE TO BE FOUND DEEP WITHIN THE FOUR CLUSTERED WALLS OF DEMON CASTLE WHERE MORLOCK THE WIZARDS STANDS DEFIANTLY BEFORE THE MIRROR OF TRUTH...
TOO LONG HAVE I GONE UNAVENGED...TOO LONG HAVE YOU SLIPPED TWIXT MY GRASP BUT NOW YOU ARE MINE.
SO NEAR? IT SEEMS AS IF FATE REWARDS ME FOR MY INFINITE PATIENCE.
NOW TO EXACT MY BITTER-SWEET REVENGE.
MIRROR OF TRUTH...REVEAL UNTO ME THE WHEREABOUTS OF MY COWARDLY FOE.
OH RIDES CASSANDRA OF THE SEVENTH WIND AS BEAUTIFUL AND GENTLE AS CAN BE...
ENOUGH, MYNSTREL. I FEAR THAN EVEN YOUR SOFT RHYMES MAY ALERT THE ONE I SEEK TO OUR PRESENCE.
INDEED, EVEN AS WE SPEAK IN HUSHED TONES, WE DRAW EVEN CLOSER TO OUR DESTINATION.
AND SUDDENLY THE SKIES TURN AN EBONY BLACK AS LIVING STORM CLOUDS ROLL QUICKLY OVER CASSANDRA AND HER VALIANT PARTY...
WHAT IS THIS MADNESS? MERE SECONDS BEFORE IT WAS CLEAR AS SPRING.
THERE IS NO PLACE TO HIDE FROM MORLOCK'S LIGHTNING...NO WHERE TO RUN 'TIL MY VENGEANCE IS DONE.
I KNOW NOT REASON FOR THIS COWARDLY ATTACK...
TO COVER, MY FRIENDS. RACE FOR COVER!
BUT...NONE MAY ATTACK CASSANDRA WITHOUT FEELING HER MIGHT IN RETURN.

CASSANDRA REACHES TOWARDS HER HORSES HILTER AND DRAWS FROM IT A SWORD ABLAZE WITH EMERALD FIRE...
LET THOSE WHO MOCK CASSANDRA. FOR NONE CAN FACE THE INFINITE POWER OF BANSHEE, THE FLAMING SWORD, AND SURVIVE.
AN UNEARTHLY SCREAM RAGES FORTH FROM THE FLAMING SWORD, AND THEN...
BY FRELM! MIGHTY SWORD, FLAME ON FOR YOUR MISTRESS. DESTROY...DESTROY!!
TWIN BEAMS OF MYSTIC ENERGIES MEET HIGH ABOVE THE SOILED CORRIDORS OF EARTH AND BURST INTO MULTI-COLORED LUMINESCENCE THAT BATHES THE YOUNG PLANET IN A HARSH APOCOLYPTIC GLOW...
LET THE FLAMES OF CERBERUS DO EACH OTHER BATTLE, WIZARD.
BUT YOU I WISH TO MEET IN FLESH, NOT SPIRIT.
COME FORTH FROM YOUR CONCEALMENT, OR HENCEFORTH BE KNOWN AS COWARD.
FOOLISH WOMAN YOU FRIGHTEN ME NOT.
YOUR POWERS ARE AS OF WORMS COMPARED TO MINE. YOUR WEAPONS ARE MEANINGLESS...INEFFEC- TUAL ORNAMENTATION.
DO NOT ATTEMPT TO FRIGHTEN ME, WOMAN. FOR YOU CAN NOT.

AND THEN, AS IF MOCKING THE QUEEN OF THE SEVENTH WIND...
HA! HA! HA! HA! HA!
ARGHHH!
AND THERE IS ONLY SILENCE...
AT LAST, WITHIN MY REACH THE ONE FOR WHOM I HAVE SEARCHED SO LONG.
ATLANTIS, YOU SHALL BE AVENGED! YOUR MURDERER IS HERE!
THE PURPLE SHROUD THAT LAY PRESSED AGAINST CASSANDRA'S MIND LIFTS, AND HER EYES SLOWLY OPEN TO SEE...
WHERE...?
THE JUNGLE STILL SURROUNDS ME LIKE SOME DARK FORBODING NIGHTMARE!
DAMON, YOU ARE THERE, BUT...
MYNSTREL!! WHERE IS MYNSTREL?
AND THEN, SUDDENLY CASSANDRA'S EYES GO BLANK, HER MIND EXPLODES, AND SHE SEEMS AS IF LINKED TO SOME FORCE AS YET UNKNOWN...
YES! I HEAR YOU, CASSANDRA. I HEAR YOU CRYING.
I HAVE NOT FORGOTTEN YOU!
AND AS SUDDENLY AT IT CAME, THE STRANGE COUNTERENCE IS GONE...
DAMON SHE IS NEARBY.
OUR QUEST IS ENDING AT LAST!
WE MUST HURRY TO THE CASTLE. FOR NOT ONLY MAY WE RESCUE YOUNG MYNSTREL, BUT CASSANDRA CAN AGAIN BE WITH US!
THE CASTLE. HE MUST HAVE BEEN TAKEN THERE.
BUT WHY MYNSTREL...A MERE SINGER OF SONGS?
COULD IT BE THAT MORLOCK WAS NOT AFTER ME AT ALL, DAMON, BUT THAT MYNSTREL WAS HIS TARGET?
WHY? WHY?
I COME, MY GEMINI...I COME TO BE WHOLE WITH YOU.

ENTER NOT, MISTRESS. I SENSE DISASTER!
SO, DAMON, THE DOOMSAYER, SPEAKS! FEAR NOT FOR ME, OLD FRIEND!
WORRY ONLY FOR MORLOCK, FOR HE HAS INCURRED THE WRATH OF CASSANDRA.
THIS CANNOT BE. ALL MY POWERS HAVE YET TO OPEN THIS SIMPLE DOOR.
ARE MORLOCK'S POWERS INFINITE?
IS THERE NOTHING WE CAN DO, DAMON?
CASSANDRA MOVES FROM BEFORE THE IMPASSABLE DOOR AS DAMON STARES AT IT, HIS STAFF EXTENDED. FOR LONG MOMENTS NOTHING HAPPENS, AND THEN...
IT FALLS AS BUTTER MELTS BEFORE A HEATED BLADE.
THERE IS STILL SO MUCH ABOUT YOU, DAMON OF WHICH I KNOW NOT!
BUT COME, WE MUST RESCUE MINSTREL.
CASSANDRA RACES THROUGH THE WINDING CORRIDORS OF DEMON CASTLE, AND THEN, SUDDENLY, AS IF FROM NOWHERE...
BY FRELM! WHAT ARE THESE HORRORS THAT STAND BEFORE ME?
ARE THEY SOME BLASPHEMOUS PERVERTED REALITY, OR A NIGHTMARISH ILLUSION?
WHICHEVER THEY SHALL NOT STOP CASSANDRA!

THEY ARE REAL, AS REAL AS THEY LOOK. INDEED IT TOOK A SORCERER MIGHTIER THAN MYSELF TO CONJURE THEM!
BUT... CASSANDRA SHALL STILL DEFEAT THEM!
THE INNER FORCE THAT IS CASSANDRA PUSHES HER WAY THROUGH AS SHE AND BANSHEE THE FLAMING SWORD OPEN A PATH AGAINST THE MYRIAD OF MINDLESS CREATURE -- THAT TEAR AT HER...
I BEGIN TO WEAKEN...THESE BEASTS DRAW BLOOD, BUT STILL I MUST FIGHT.
I MUST... I MUST!!
I MUST!!

YOU HAVE RUN A LONG JOURNEY, MYNSTREL. BUT NOW I HAVE YOU HERE, BEFORE ME, AND YOU SHALL PAY DEARLY FOR YOUR CRIMES.
REMOVE YOUR SPELL FROM HIM, WIZARD, OR FEEL WRATH!
BLOOD DRIPS FROM YOUR BODY, WOMAN. YOU ARE WEAK, TIRED, AND YET YOU THREATEN ME!
YOU HAVE COURAGE, BUT YOU ARE A FOOL!
WITH THE SPEED OF AN ENRAGED CAT, CASSANDRA STRIKE OUT...
WHERE IS SHE, WIZARD? WHAT HAVE YOU DONE WITH CASSANDRA?
SPEAK NOW OR PERISH!
YOU TALK IN RIDDLES, MAD ONE. YOU ARE CASSANDRA!
I AM RECEIVING MY STRENGTH THROUGH HER. SHE IS NEAR.
WHERE, DAMNED ONE? WHERE?
TOO LATE, THE CRIMSON BEAM STRUCK HIM!
BUT THAT STILL SHALL NOT STOP ME FROM LEARNING WHAT I WANT!
IF HE CANNOT SPEAK TO ME, HIS MIND CAN STILL REVEAL CASSANDRA'S PRESENCE...

CASSANDRA STANDS BEFORE THE UNCONSCIOUS FORM OF MORLOCK, IMPERIAL WIZARD OF ATLANTIS, AND...
MAY THE GREAT FRELM OPEN YOUR MIND TO ME. LET ALL THAT IS WITHIN BE SHARED OPEN WIDE YOUR KNOWLEDGE!
AND THEN, CASSANDRA FINDS HERSELF BEFORE THE THRESHOLD OF CONSCIOUSNESS, WITHIN THE MIND OF MORLOCK...
I MUST GO DEEPER INTO HIS UNCONSCIOUS TO FIND WHAT I SEEK.
SHE IS THERE... FURTHER ON!
I MUST GET TO HER... RESCUE HER...
HOLD STILL, CASSANDRA. I COME FOR YOU.
WHERE ARE YOU, CASSANDRA ...SPEAK TO ME!
GIVE ME YOUR HAND SO THAT I MAY FREE YOU!
SAVE ME, CASSANDRA... SAVE ME!
THEY'RE COMING AGAIN ...COMING TO TORTURE ME! HELP ME!
WHERE ARE YOU? TELL ME WHERE YOU ARE!
THEY'RE COMING FOR ME, CASSANDRA ...COMING!
SAVE ME... WE ARE TWO... BUT WE ARE ONE... SAVE ME, CASSANDRA... SAVE ME...
WHAT HAPPENED? EVERYTHING'S BLACK!!

THEY SAY THAT SOMEWHERE WITHIN ETERNITY STANDS THE QUESTION, "WHY?" REACHING OUT TOWARDS INFINITY, SEARCHING FOR THE FINAL ANSWER SO THAT IT MAY REST IN PEACE. AND SOMEWHERE IN THE VASTNESS THAT IS EVERYTHING, THE TRODDEN GLOBE KNOWN AS EARTH REVOLVES. AND ON THIS DUST-FILLED BOWL STANDS THREE PERSONS. ALL THREE, ENIGMAS...ALL THREE SEEM TO CRY OUT AND ASK, "WHY?" AND ALL THREE RECEIVE ONLY THE FAINTEST CLUE AS TO THEIR REASON OF BEING!

THE COMET

BY W.E.B. DU BOIS

He stood a moment on the steps of the bank, watching the human river that swirled down Broadway. Few noticed him. Few ever noticed him save in a way that stung. He was outside the world—"nothing!" as he said bitterly. Bits of the words of the walkers came to him.

"The comet?"

"The comet—»

Everybody was talking of it. Even the president, as he entered, smiled patronizingly at him, and asked:

"Well, Jim, are you scared?"

"No," said the messenger shortly.

"I thought we'd journeyed through the comet's tail once," broke in the junior clerk affably.

"Oh, that was Halley's," said the president; "this is a new comet, quite a stranger, they say—wonderful, wonderful! I saw it last night. Oh, by the way, Jim," turning again to the messenger, "I want you to go down into the lower vaults today."

The messenger followed the president silently. Of course, they wanted *him* to go down to the lower vaults. It was too dangerous for more valuable men. He smiled grimly and listened.

"Everything of value has been moved out since the water began to seep in," said the president; "but we miss two volumes of old records. Suppose you nose around down there,—it isn't very pleasant, I suppose."

"Not very," said the messenger, as he walked out.

"Well, Jim, the tail of the new comet hits us at noon this time," said the vault clerk, as he passed over the keys; but the messenger passed silently down the stairs.

Down he went beneath Broadway, where the dim light filtered through the feet of hurrying men; down to the dark basement beneath; down into the blackness and silence beneath that lowest cavern. Here with his dark lantern he groped in the bowels of the earth, under the world.

He drew a long breath as he threw back the last great iron door and stepped into the fetid slime within. Here at last was peace, and he groped moodily forward. A great rat leaped past him and cobwebs crept across his face. He felt carefully around the room, shelf by shelf, on the muddied floor, and in crevice and corner. Nothing. Then he went back to the far end, where somehow the wall felt different. He sounded and pushed and pried. Nothing. He started away. Then something brought him back. He was sounding and working again when suddenly the whole black wall swung as on mighty hinges, and blackness yawned beyond. He peered in; it was evidently a secret vault—some hiding place of the old bank unknown in newer times. He entered hesitatingly. It was a long, narrow room with shelves, and at the far end, an old iron chest. On a high shelf lay the two missing volumes of records, and others. He put them carefully aside and stepped to the chest. It was old, strong, and rusty. He looked at the vast and old-fashioned lock and flashed his light on the hinges. They were deeply incrusted with rust. Looking about, he found a bit of iron and began to pry. The rust had eaten a hundred years, and it had gone deep. Slowly, wearily, the old lid lifted, and with a last, low groan lay bare its treasure—and he saw the dull sheen of gold!

"Boom!"

A low, grinding, reverberating crash struck upon his ear. He started up and looked about. All was black and still. He groped for his light and swung it about him. Then he knew! The great stone door had swung to. He forgot the gold and looked death squarely in the face. Then with a sigh he went methodically to work. The cold sweat stood on his forehead; but he searched, pounded, pushed, and worked until after what seemed endless hours his hand struck a cold bit of metal and the great door swung again harshly on its hinges, and then, striking against something soft and heavy, stopped. He had just room to squeeze through. There lay the body of the vault clerk, cold and stiff. He stared at it, and then felt sick and nauseated. The air seemed unaccountably foul, with a strong, peculiar odor. He stepped forward, clutched at the air, and fell fainting across the corpse.

He awoke with a sense of horror, leaped from the body, and groped up the stairs, calling to the guard. The watchman sat as if asleep, with the gate swinging free. With one glance at him the messenger hurried up to the sub-vault. In vain he called to the guards. His voice echoed and re-echoed weirdly. Up into the great basement he rushed. Here another guard lay prostrate on his face, cold and still. A fear arose in the messenger's heart. He dashed up to the cellar floor, up into the bank. The stillness of death lay everywhere and everywhere bowed, bent, and stretched the silent forms of men. The messenger paused and glanced about. He was not a man easily moved; but the sight was appalling! "Robbery and murder," he whispered slowly to himself as he saw the twisted, oozing mouth of the president where he lay half-buried on his desk. Then a new thought seized him: If they found him here alone—with all this money and all these dead men—what would his life be worth?

He glanced about, tiptoed cautiously to a side door, and again looked behind. Quietly he turned the latch and stepped out into Wall Street.

How silent the street was! Not a soul was stirring, and yet it was high-noon—Wall Street? Broadway? He glanced almost wildly up and down, then across the street, and as he looked, a sickening horror froze in his limbs. With a choking cry of utter fright he lunged, leaned giddily against the cold building, and stared helplessly at the sight.

In the great stone doorway a hundred men and women and children lay crushed and twisted and jammed, forced into that great, gaping doorway like refuse in a can—as if in one wild, frantic rush to safety, they had rushed and ground themselves to death. Slowly the messenger crept along the walls, wetting his parched mouth and trying to comprehend, stilling the tremor in his limbs and the rising terror in his heart. He met a business man, silk-hatted and frock-coated, who had crept, too, along that smooth wall and stood now stone dead with wonder written on his lips. The messenger turned his eyes hastily away and sought the curb. A woman leaned wearily against the signpost, her head bowed motionless on her lace and silken bosom. Before her stood a street car, silent, and within—but the messenger but glanced and hurried on. A grimy newsboy sat in the gutter with the "last edition" in his uplifted hand: "Danger!" screamed its black headlines. "Warnings wired around the world. The Comet's tail sweeps past us at noon. Deadly gases expected. Close doors and windows. Seek the cellar." The messenger read and staggered on. Far out from a window above, a girl lay with gasping face and sleevelets on her arms. On a store step sat a little, sweet-faced girl looking upward toward the skies, and in the carriage by her lay—but the messenger looked no longer. The cords gave way—the terror burst in his veins, and with one great, gasping cry he sprang desperately forward and ran,—ran as only the frightened run, shrieking and fighting the air until with one last wail of pain he sank on the grass of Madison Square and lay prone and still.

When he rose, he gave no glance at the still and silent forms on the benches, but, going to a fountain, bathed his face; then hiding himself in a corner away from the drama of death, he quietly gripped himself and thought the thing through: The comet had swept the earth and this was the end. Was everybody dead? He must search and see.

He knew that he must steady himself and keep calm, or he would go insane. First he must go to a restaurant. He walked up Fifth Avenue to a famous hostelry and entered its gorgeous, ghost-haunted halls. He beat back the nausea, and, seizing a tray from dead hands, hurried into the street and ate ravenously, hiding to keep out the sights.

"Yesterday, they would not have served me," he whispered, as he forced the food down.

Then he started up the street,—looking, peering, telephoning, ringing alarms; silent, silent all. Was nobody—nobody—he dared not think the thought and hurried on.

Suddenly he stopped still. He had forgotten. My God! How could he have forgotten? He must rush to the subway—then he almost laughed. No—a car; if he could find a Ford. He saw one. Gently he lifted off its burden, and took his place on the seat. He tested the throttle. There was gas. He glided off, shivering, and drove up the street. Everywhere stood, leaned, lounged, and lay the dead, in grim and awful silence. On he ran past an automobile, wrecked and overturned; past another, filled with a gay party whose smiles yet lingered on their death-struck lips; on past crowds and groups of cars, pausing by dead policemen; at 42nd Street he had to detour to Park Avenue to avoid the dead congestion. He came back on Fifth Avenue at 57th and flew past the Plaza and by the park with its hushed babies and silent throng, until as he was rushing past 72nd Street he heard a sharp cry, and saw a living form leaning wildly out an upper window. He gasped. The human voice sounded in his ears like the voice of God.

"Hello—hello—help, in God's name!" wailed the woman. "There's a dead girl in here and a man and—and see yonder dead men lying in the street and dead horses—for the love of God go and bring the officers—" And the words trailed off into hysterical tears.

He wheeled the car in a sudden circle, running over the still body of a child and leaping on the curb. Then he rushed up the steps and tried the door and rang violently. There was a long pause, but at last the heavy door swung back. They stared a moment in silence. She had not noticed before that he was a Negro. He had not thought of her as white. She was a woman of perhaps twenty-five—rarely beautiful and richly gowned, with darkly-golden hair, and jewels. Yesterday, he thought with bitterness, she would scarcely have looked at him twice. He would have been dirt beneath her silken feet. She stared at him. Of all the sorts of men she had pictured as coming to her rescue she had not dreamed of one like him. Not that he was not human, but he dwelt in a world so far from hers, so infinitely far, that he seldom even entered her thought. Yet as she looked at him curiously he seemed quite commonplace and usual. He was a tall, dark workingman of the better class, with a sensitive face trained to stolidity and a poor man's clothes and hands. His face was soft and slow and his manner at once cold and nervous, like fires long banked, but not out.

So a moment each paused and gauged the other; then the thought of the dead world without rushed in and they started toward each other.

"What has happened?" she cried. "Tell me! Nothing stirs. All is silence! I see the dead strewn before my window as winnowed by the breath of God,—and see—" She dragged him through great, silken hangings to where, beneath the sheen of mahogany and silver, a little French maid lay stretched in quiet, everlasting sleep, and near her a butler lay prone in his livery.

The tears streamed down the woman's cheeks and she clung to his arm until the perfume of her breath swept his face and he felt the tremors racing through her body.

"I had been shut up in my dark room developing pictures of the comet which I took last night; when I came out—I saw the dead!

"What has happened?" she cried again.

He answered slowly:

"Something—comet or devil—swept across the earth this morning and—many are dead!"

"Many? Very many?"

"I have searched and I have seen no other living soul but you."

She gasped and they stared at each other.

«My—father!" she whispered.

"Where is he?"

"He started for the office."

"Where is it?"

"In the Metropolitan Tower."

"Leave a note for him here and come."

Then he stopped.

"No," he said firmly—"first, we must go—to Harlem.»

"Harlem!" she cried. Then she understood. She tapped her foot at first impatiently. She looked back and shuddered. Then she came resolutely down the steps.

"There's a swifter car in the garage in the court," she said.

"I don't know how to drive it," he said.

"I do," she answered.

In ten minutes they were flying to Harlem on the wind. The Stutz rose and raced like an airplane. They took the turn at 110th Street on two wheels and slipped with a shriek into 135th.

He was gone but a moment. Then he returned, and his face was gray. She did not look, but said:

"You have lost—somebody?"

"I have lost—everybody," he said, simply—"unless—»

He ran back and was gone several minutes—hours they seemed to her.

"Everybody," he said, and he walked slowly back with something film-like in his hand which he stuffed into his pocket.

"I'm afraid I was selfish," he said. But already the car was moving toward the park among the dark and lined dead of Harlem—the brown, still faces, the knotted hands, the homely garments, and the silence—the wild and haunting silence. Out of the park, and down Fifth Avenue they whirled. In and out among the dead they slipped and quivered, needing no sound of bell or horn, until the great, square Metropolitan Tower hove in sight. Gently he laid the dead elevator boy aside; the car shot upward. The door of the office stood open. On the threshold lay the stenographer, and, staring at her, sat the dead clerk. The inner office was empty, but a note lay on the desk, folded and addressed but unsent:

Dear Daughter:

I've gone for a hundred mile spin in Fred's new Mercedes. Shall not be back before dinner. I'll bring Fred with me.

J.B.H.

"Come," she cried nervously. "We must search the city."

Up and down, over and across, back again—on went that ghostly search. Everywhere was silence and death—death and silence! They hunted from Madison Square to Spuyten Duyvel; they rushed across the Williamsburg Bridge; they swept over Brooklyn; from the Battery and Morningside Heights they scanned the river. Silence, silence everywhere, and no human sign. Haggard and bedraggled they puffed a third time slowly down Broadway, under the broiling sun, and at last stopped. He sniffed the air. An odor—a smell—and with the shifting breeze a sickening stench filled their nostrils and brought its awful warning. The girl settled back helplessly in her seat.

"What can we do?" she cried.

It was his turn now to take the lead, and he did it quickly.

"The long distance telephone—the telegraph and the cable—night rockets and then—flight!"

She looked at him now with strength and confidence. He did not look like men, as she had always pictured men; but he acted like one and she was content. In fifteen minutes they were at the central telephone exchange. As they came to the door he stepped quickly before her and pressed her gently back as he closed it. She heard him moving to and fro, and knew his burdens—the poor, little burdens he bore. When she entered, he was alone in the room. The grim switchboard flashed its metallic face in cryptic, sphinx-like immobility. She seated herself on a stool and donned the bright earpiece. She looked at the mouthpiece. She had never looked at one so closely before. It was wide and black, pimpled with usage; inert; dead; almost sarcastic in its unfeeling curves. It looked—she beat back the thought—but it looked,—it persisted in looking like—she turned her head and found herself alone. One moment she was terrified; then she thanked him silently for his delicacy and turned resolutely, with a quick intaking of breath.

"Hello!" she called in low tones. She was calling to the world. The world *must* answer. Would the world *answer*? Was the world—

Silence!

She had spoken too low.

"Hello!" she cried, full-voiced.

She listened. Silence! Her heart beat quickly. She cried in clear, distinct, loud tones: "Hello—hello—hello!"

What was that whirring? Surely—no—was it the click of a receiver?

She bent close, she moved the pegs in the holes, and called and called, until her voice rose almost to a shriek, and her heart hammered. It was as if she had heard the last flicker of creation, and the evil was silence. Her voice dropped to a sob. She sat stupidly staring into the black and sarcastic mouthpiece, and the thought came again. Hope lay dead within her. Yes, the cable and the rockets remained; but the world—she could not frame the thought or say the word. It was too mighty—too terrible! She turned toward the door with a new fear in her heart. For the first time she seemed to realize that she was alone in the world with a stranger, with something more than a stranger,—with a man alien in blood and culture—unknown, perhaps unknowable. It was awful! She must escape—she must fly; he must not see her again. Who knew what awful thoughts—

She gathered her silken skirts deftly about her young, smooth limbs—listened, and glided into a sidehall. A moment she shrank back: the hall lay filled with dead women; then she leaped to the door and tore at it, with bleeding fingers, until it swung wide. She looked out. He was standing at the top of the alley,—silhouetted, tall and black, motionless. Was he looking at her or away? She did not know—she did not care. She simply leaped and ran—ran until she found herself alone amid the dead and the tall ramparts of towering buildings.

She stopped. She was alone. Alone! Alone on the streets—alone in the city—perhaps alone in the world! There crept in upon her the sense of deception—of creeping hands behind her back—of silent, moving things she could not see,—of voices hushed in fearsome conspiracy. She looked behind and sideways, started at strange sounds and heard still stranger, until every nerve within her stood sharp and quivering, stretched to scream at the barest touch. She whirled and flew back, whimpering like a child, until she found that narrow alley again and the dark, silent figure silhouetted at the top. She stopped and rested; then she walked silently toward him, looked at him timidly; but he said nothing as he handed her into the car. Her voice caught as she whispered:

«Not—that."

And he answered slowly: "No—not that!"

They climbed into the car. She bent forward on the wheel and sobbed, with great, dry, quivering sobs, as they flew toward the cable office on the east side, leaving the world of wealth and prosperity for the world of poverty and work. In the world behind them were death and silence, grave and grim, almost cynical, but always decent; here it was hideous. It clothed itself in every ghastly form of terror, struggle, hate, and suffering. It lay wreathed in crime and squalor, greed and lust. Only in its dread and awful silence was it like to death everywhere.

Yet as the two, flying and alone, looked upon the horror of the world, slowly, gradually, the sense of all-enveloping death deserted them. They seemed to move in a world silent and asleep,—not dead. They moved in quiet reverence, lest somehow they wake these sleeping forms who had, at last, found peace. They moved in some solemn, world-wide *Friedhof*, above which some mighty arm had waved its magic wand. All nature slept until—until, and quick with the same startling thought, they looked into each other's eyes—he, ashen, and she, crimson, with unspoken thought. To both, the vision of a mighty beauty—of vast, unspoken things, swelled in their souls; but they put it away.

Great, dark coils of wire came up from the earth and down from the sun and entered this low lair of witchery. The gathered lightnings of the world centered here, binding with beams of light the ends of the earth. The doors gaped on the gloom within. He paused on the threshold.

"Do you know the code?" she asked.

"I know the call for help—we used it formerly at the bank."

She hardly heard. She heard the lapping of the waters far below,—the dark and restless waters—the cold and luring waters, as they called. He stepped within. Slowly she walked to the wall, where the water called below, and stood and waited. Long she waited, and he did not come. Then with a start she saw him, too, standing beside the black waters. Slowly he removed his coat and stood there silently. She walked quickly to him and laid her hand on his arm. He did not start or look. The waters lapped on in luring, deadly rhythm. He pointed down to the waters, and said quietly:

"The world lies beneath the waters now—may I go?"

She looked into his stricken, tired face, and a great pity surged within her heart. She answered in a voice clear and calm, "No."

Upward they turned toward life again, and he seized the wheel. The world was darkening to twilight, and a great, gray pall was falling mercifully and gently on the sleeping dead. The ghastly glare of reality seemed replaced with the dream of some vast romance. The girl lay silently back, as the motor whizzed along, and looked half-consciously for the elf-queen to wave life into this dead world again. She forgot to wonder at the quickness with which he had learned to drive her car. It seemed natural. And then as they whirled and swung into Madison Square and at the door of the Metropolitan Tower she gave a low cry, and her eyes were great! Perhaps she had seen the elf-queen?

The man led her to the elevator of the tower and deftly they ascended. In her father's office they gathered rugs and chairs, and he wrote a note and laid it on the desk; then they ascended to the roof and he made her comfortable. For a while she rested and sank to dreamy somnolence, watching the worlds above and wondering. Below lay the dark shadows of the city and afar was the shining of the sea. She glanced at him timidly as he set food before her and took a shawl and wound her in it, touching her reverently, yet tenderly. She looked up at him with thankfulness in her eyes, eating what he served. He watched the city. She watched him. He seemed very human,—very near now.

"Have you had to work hard?" she asked softly.

"Always," he said.

"I have always been idle," she said. "I was rich."

"I was poor," he almost echoed.

"The rich and the poor are met together," she began, and he finished:

"The Lord is the Maker of them all."

"Yes," she said slowly; "and how foolish our human distinctions seem—now," looking down to the great dead city stretched below, swimming in unlightened shadows.

"Yes—I was not—human, yesterday," he said.

She looked at him. "And your people were not my people," she said; "but today—" She paused. He was a man,—no more; but he was in some larger sense a gentleman,—sensitive, kindly, chivalrous, everything save his hands and—his face. Yet yesterday—

"Death, the leveler!" he muttered.

"And the revealer," she whispered gently, rising to her feet with great eyes. He turned away, and after fumbling a moment sent a rocket into the darkening air. It arose, shrieked, and flew up, a slim path of light, and scattering its stars abroad, dropped on the city below. She scarcely noticed it. A vision of the world had risen before her. Slowly the mighty prophecy of her destiny overwhelmed her. Above the dead past hovered the Angel of Annunciation. She was no mere woman. She was neither high nor low, white nor black, rich nor poor. She was primal woman; mighty mother of all men to come and Bride of Life. She looked upon the man beside her and forgot all else but his manhood, his strong, vigorous manhood—his sorrow and sacrifice. She saw him glorified. He was no longer a thing apart, a creature below, a strange outcast of another clime and blood, but her Brother Humanity incarnate, Son of God and great All-Father of the race to be.

He did not glimpse the glory in her eyes, but stood looking outward toward the sea and sending rocket after rocket into the unanswering darkness. Dark-purple clouds lay banked and billowed in the west. Behind them and all around, the heavens glowed in dim, weird radiance that suffused the darkening world and made almost a minor music. Suddenly, as though gathered back in some vast hand, the great cloud-curtain fell away. Low on the horizon lay a long, white star—mystic, wonderful! And from it fled upward to the pole, like some wan bridal veil, a pale, wide sheet of flame that lighted all the world and dimmed the stars.

In fascinated silence the man gazed at the heavens and dropped his rockets to the floor. Memories of memories stirred to life in the dead recesses of his mind. The shackles seemed to rattle and fall from his soul. Up from the crass and crushing and cringing of his caste leaped the lone majesty of kings long dead. He arose within the shadows, tall, straight, and stern, with power in his eyes and ghostly scepters hovering to his grasp. It was as though some mighty Pharaoh lived again, or curled Assyrian lord. He turned and looked upon the lady, and found her gazing straight at him.

Silently, immovably, they saw each other face to face—eye to eye. Their souls lay naked to the night. It was not lust; it was not love—it was some vaster, mightier thing that needed neither touch of body nor thrill of soul. It was a thought divine, splendid.

Slowly, noiselessly, they moved toward each other—the heavens above, the seas around, the city grim and dead below. He loomed from out the velvet shadows vast and dark. Pearl-white and slender, she shone beneath the stars. She stretched her jeweled hands abroad. He lifted up his mighty arms, and they cried each to the other, almost with one voice, "The world is dead."

"Long live the—»

"Honk! Honk!" Hoarse and sharp the cry of a motor drifted clearly up from the silence below. They started backward with a cry and gazed upon each other with eyes that faltered and fell, with blood that boiled.

"Honk! Honk! Honk! Honk!" came the mad cry again, and almost from their feet a rocket blazed into the air and scattered its stars upon them. She covered her eyes with her hands, and her shoulders heaved. He dropped and bowed, groped blindly on his knees about the floor. A blue flame spluttered lazily after an age, and she heard the scream of an answering rocket as it flew.

Then they stood still as death, looking to opposite ends of the earth.

«Clang—crash—clang!"

The roar and ring of swift elevators shooting upward from below made the great tower tremble. A murmur and babel of voices swept in upon the night. All over the once dead city the lights blinked, flickered, and flamed; and then with a sudden clanging of doors the entrance to the platform was filled with men, and one with white and flying hair rushed to the girl and lifted her to his breast. "My daughter!" he sobbed.

Behind him hurried a younger, comelier man, carefully clad in motor costume, who bent above the girl with passionate solicitude and gazed into her staring eyes until they narrowed and dropped and her face flushed deeper and deeper crimson.

"Julia," he whispered; "my darling, I thought you were gone forever."

She looked up at him with strange, searching eyes.

"Fred," she murmured, almost vaguely, "is the world—gone?"

"Only New York," he answered; "it is terrible—awful! You know,—but you, how did you escape—how have you endured this horror? Are you well? Unharmed?"

"Unharmed!" she said.

"And this man here?" he asked, encircling her drooping form with one arm and turning toward the Negro. Suddenly he stiffened and his hand flew to his hip. "Why!" he snarled. "It's—a—nigger—Julia! Has he—has he dared—»

She lifted her head and looked at her late companion curiously and then dropped her eyes with a sigh.

"He has dared—all, to rescue me," she said quietly, "and I—thank him—much." But she did not look at him again. As the couple turned away, the father drew a roll of bills from his pockets.

"Here, my good fellow," he said, thrusting the money into the man's hands, "take that,—what's your name?"

"Jim Davis," came the answer, hollow-voiced.

"Well, Jim, I thank you. I've always liked your people. If you ever want a job, call on me." And they were gone.

The crowd poured up and out of the elevators, talking and whispering.

"Who was it?"

"Are they alive?"

"How many?"

"Two!"

"Who was saved?"

"A white girl and a nigger—there she goes."

"A nigger? Where is he? Let's lynch the damned—»

"Shut up—he's all right-he saved her."

"Saved hell! He had no business—»

"Here he comes."

Into the glare of the electric lights the colored man moved slowly, with the eyes of those that walk and sleep.

"Well, what do you think of that?" cried a bystander; "of all New York, just a white girl and a nigger!"

The colored man heard nothing. He stood silently beneath the glare of the light, gazing at the money in his hand and shrinking as he gazed; slowly he put his other hand into his pocket and brought out a baby's filmy cap, and gazed again. A woman mounted to the platform and looked about, shading her eyes. She was brown, small, and toil-worn, and in one arm lay the corpse of a dark baby. The crowd parted and her eyes fell on the colored man; with a cry she tottered toward him.

«Jim!»

He whirled and, with a sob of joy, caught her in his arms.

THE END

"THE MOST EFFECTIVE WAY TO DESTROY PEOPLE IS TO DENY AND OBLITERATE THEIR OWN UNDERSTANDING OF THEIR HISTORY."

— GEORGE ORWELL

"IT IS NOT THE CRITIC WHO COUNTS; NOT THE MAN WHO POINTS OUT HOW THE STRONG MAN STUMBLES, OR WHERE THE DOER OF DEEDS COULD HAVE DONE THEM BETTER. THE CREDIT BELONGS TO THE MAN WHO IS ACTUALLY IN THE ARENA, WHOSE FACE IS MARRED BY DUST AND SWEAT AND BLOOD; WHO STRIVES VALIANTLY; WHO ERRS, WHO COMES SHORT AGAIN AND AGAIN, BECAUSE THERE IS NO EFFORT WITHOUT ERROR AND SHORTCOMING; BUT WHO DOES ACTUALLY STRIVE TO DO THE DEEDS; WHO KNOWS GREAT ENTHUSIASMS, THE GREAT DEVOTIONS; WHO SPENDS HIMSELF IN A WORTHY CAUSE; WHO AT THE BEST KNOWS IN THE END THE TRIUMPH OF HIGH ACHIEVEMENT, AND WHO AT THE WORST, IF HE FAILS, AT LEAST FAILS WHILE DARING GREATLY, SO THAT HIS PLACE SHALL NEVER BE WITH THOSE COLD AND TIMID SOULS WHO NEITHER KNOW VICTORY NOR DEFEAT."

— THEODORE ROOSEVELT

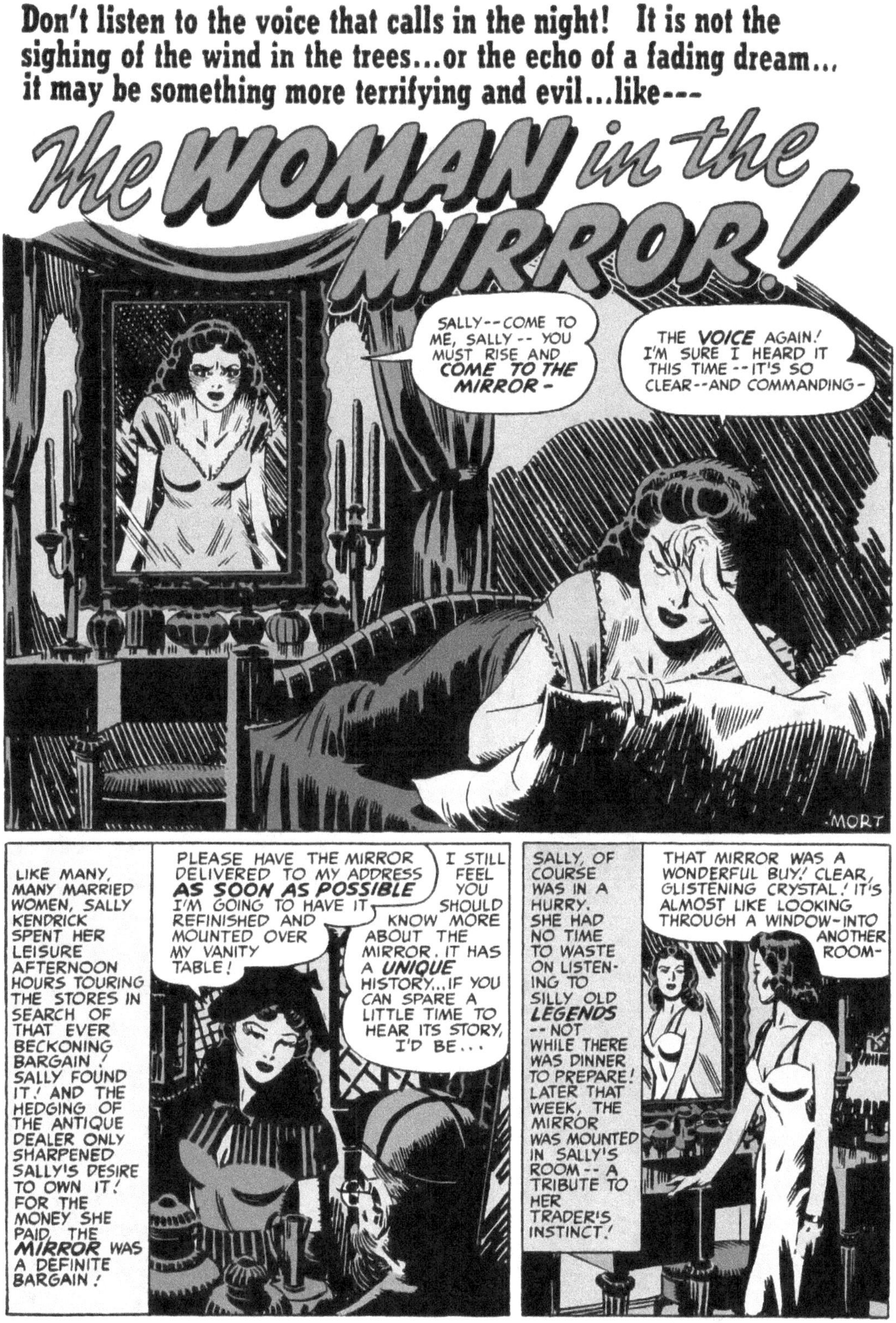

Don't listen to the voice that calls in the night!   It is not the sighing of the wind in the trees...or the echo of a fading dream... it may be something more terrifying and evil...like---

The WOMAN in the MIRROR!

HOW STRANGE! I'M NOT FROWNING...YET MY REFLECTION SEEMS TO BE...OH...BUT THAT'S RIDICULOUS!

"OF COURSE! IT WAS PROBABLY THE LIGHTING IN THE ROOM! THAT WAS IT! THE LIGHTING! LIGHT OF OFTEN PLAYS TRICKS ON THE SENSES! IT WAS THE LOGICAL EXPLANATION! BUT SOMETHING INSIDE SALLY DIDN'T ACCEPT IT!
IT'S A VERY LOVELY FACE! AND, I DON'T BLAME YOU FOR STARING AT IT! BUT IT'S TIME WE WERE ON OUR WAY, DARLING!
OH, DEAR! I'M SORRY! I MUST HAVE BEEN DAY DREAMING!

LET'S GET STARTED SALLY! YOU MAY BE THE GUEST OF HONOR, BUT IT'S STILL IMPOLITE TO KEEP THE OTHERS WAITING!
I...I'M READY! IT'S IMPOSSIBLE— IMPOSSIBLE!

"SALLY MAY AS WELL HAVE NOT ATTENDED THE PARTY FOR ALL THE ATTENTION SHE PAID TO THE FESTIVITIES...HER MIND WAS OCCUPIED WITH A PERSISTING THOUGHT...AN INCREDIBLE THOUGHT...
I'VE NEVER SEEN YOU LOOKING LOVELIER, SALLY! HOW DO YOU DO IT?
OH! IT'S YOU, HAL! I...I WAS JUST PRE-OCCUPIED!

ARE YOU SURE YOUR WIFE ISN'T IN LOVE WITH ANOTHER MAN, TOM? SHE'S BEEN ACTING MIGHTY STRANGE TONIGHT!
HER MIND'S PROBABLY ON THE MONTH'S BUDGET!

"SALLY WAS THE BUTT OF MORE THAN ONE GOOD-NATURED JIBE THAT EVENING.. SHE NEITHER HEARD NOR ANSWERED ANY OF IT! ONLY UPON HER RETURN HOME DID SALLY BECOME AWARE OF THINGS! ESPECIALLY THE MIRROR ...AND THE INTENSE, HYPNOTIC STARE OF HER REFLECTION!

2

"THERE WAS SOMETHING ABOUT HER MIRROR IMAGE WHICH DISTURBED SALLY! A SUBTLE, ELUSIVE IMPRESSION THAT THE IMAGE WAS A DISTINCT AND SEPARATE INDIVIDUAL... POSSESSING LIFE OF ITS OWN! SEATED AT HER VANITY BEFORE RETIRING FOR THE NIGHT, SALLY ONCE AGAIN STUDIED HER REFLECTION!

"AND ONCE AGAIN THE QEER FEELING CAME UPON SALLY ...THAT IT WAS NOT SHE WHO WAS OBSERVING HER IMAGE...*THE REFLECTION WAS STUDYING SALLY!*

"SALLY WAS TERRIBLY SHAKEN! WERE HER SENSES DECEIVING HER? WAS SHE GIVEN TO HALLUCINATIONS? FOR DAYS SHE AVOIDED THE MAGNETIC DRAW OF THE MIRROR! AFRAID OF WHAT SHE MIGHT SEE-- OF WHAT SHE MIGHT THINK! ONE NIGHT SALLY AROSE FROM HER SLEEP...IN THE DARKNESS OF HER ROOM- A VOICE WAS CALLING HER NAME!

"THE VOICE CAME FROM SOMEWHERE ON SALLY'S RIGHT...WHERE THE *MIRROR* HUNG! FEARFULLY, SALLY ROSE FROM THE BED TO INVESTIGATE! THAT WAS A MISTAKE! BUT HOW WAS SALLY TO KNOW?

"IT WAS THE IMAGE...ANIMATE AND ALIVE! WITH TRIUMPH IN ITS VOICE AND UNHOLY POWER IN ITS GLOWING EYES! EYES WHICH HELD SALLY FAST... DRAWING HER CLOSER--EVER CLOSER ...

"SALLY WAS LIKE A BIRD CAUGHT IN THE SPELL OF A COBRAS EYES! SHE FELT THE FULL IMPACT OF THE HORROR! BUT COULD NEITHER RUN NOR SCREAM! THE EYES GREW TO *MONSTROUS* SIZE! THERE WAS A SICKENING WRENCH! AND SALLY PLUNGED INTO DARK SPACE!

"SALLY SUDDENLY FELT HERSELF BEING VIGOROUSLY SHAKEN, AND SHE WOKE WITH A START! TOM STOOD FROWNING DOWN AT HER! BUT THE MIRROR! THAT DEVILISH REFLECTION! HAD IT ALL BEEN JUST A NIGHTMARE?
SALLY! WAKE UP! WAKE UP!
OH, TOM! I JUST HAD THE MOST PECULIAR DREAM... I...

IT SEEMS TO ME YOU'VE BEEN ACTING MIGHTY PECULIAR THIS PAST WEEK, SALLY! I'VE NEVER COMPLAINED, BUT THIS LAST SPENDING SPREE OF YOURS IS TOO MUCH! I CAN'T AFFORD THESE THINGS!
BUT TOM I HAVEN'T BOUGHT ANYTHING LATELY! I DON'T UNDERSTAND!
BILL

OH! YOU DON'T EH? WHAT DO YOU CALL THESE? SNAP OUT OF IT, SALLY! THIS BATCH OF BILLS DOESN'T STRIKE ME AS FUNNY!
BUT TOM! I NEVER BOUGHT THESE THINGS! I..I COULDN'T HAVE ...

"TOM GAVE UP AND STAMPED OFF... LEAVING SALLY CONFUSED AND FRIGHTENED! A WEEK'S BILLS..WITH SALLY'S SIGNATURE UNMISTAKENLY SIGNED TO THEM! A WEEK HAD PASSED! WHERE HAD SHE BEEN? WHO HAD BOUGHT THOSE THINGS? SUDDENLY SALLY KNEW!
IT WAS YOU! YOU REALLY DREW ME INTO THAT DEVIL'S MIRROR... AND TOOK MY PLACE HERE! WELL! YOU'LL NEVER DO IT AGAIN...

"THE MOCKING REFLECTION SEEMED TO GROW LARGE AND MENACING! ONCE AGAIN, SALLY LOOKED INTO THOSE EVIL, BURNING EYES... FELT THEM FASTEN ON HER BRAIN! TERROR REACHED OUT CAUGHT HER AS SHE RECOILED! SALLY VAINLY TRIED TO CRY OUT AGAINST WHAT SHE KNEW WAS HAPPENING!

"THE MIRROR HAD UNDREAMED OF DEPTHS! SALLY SENSED ITS VASTNESS WHEN SHE PASSED THROUGH!
4

"IT SEEMED LIKE SALLY WOULD DRIFT FOR ETERNITY IN THAT WORLD OF BLACK WRITHING SHADOWS! WHEN SHE CAME TO... IT WAS ONLY TO FIND HERSELF IMPRISONED IN THE MIRROR! LOOKING OUT INTO HER OWN ROOM.. NOW OCCUPIED BY ANOTHER WOMAN... A WOMAN WHO COULD HAVE BEEN HER TWIN! THE FIENDISH IMAGE!
SO YOU'RE AWAKE, ARE YOU SALLY? OR SHOULD I CALL YOU MY MIRROR IMAGE? THAT'S WHAT YOU ARE NOW, YOU KNOW! WE'VE CHANGED PLACES YOU AND I! THIS TIME FOR GOOD! I'VE WAITED CENTURIES FOR THIS CHANCE!

"SALLY WAS ALMOST CONSUMED BY THE UTTER HELPLESSNESS OF HER POSITION! BUT SHE COULD DO NOTHING! SHE WAS A PRISONER... AN ILLUSION! JUST THEN TOM ENTERED THE ROOM!
READY, SALLY?

"DON'T TOUCH HER TOM! IT'S A HELLISH MONSTER YOU HOLD IN YOUR ARMS!" THEY WERE WORDS THAT SALLY TRIED BUT COULDN'T SPEAK! OVER TOM'S SHOULDER, THE EVIL IMPOSTOR SMILED HER MOCKING SMILE!

"A MOMENT LATER SALLY WATCHED THEM LEAVE ARM IN ARM! AND SHE WAS LEFT ALONE TO DESPAIR IN THE DARKNESS! THE PROSPECT OF SPENDING AN ETERNAL EXISTENCE AS A REFLECTION SENT SALLY'S WHIRLING THOUGHTS IN SEARCH OF A PLAN TO BREAK FREE! WHEN THE EVIL ONE RETURNED THAT NIGHT, SALLY MADE HER EFFORT!
AREN'T YOU AFRAID TO GO TO SLEEP? KNOWING THAT I'M WAITING FOR YOU!
DON'T YOU DARE THREATEN ME!

I DREW YOU INTO THE MIRROR... AND BY ALL THE POWERS THAT HELPED ME DO IT... I'LL SEE THAT YOU STAY THERE!

"THAT WAS WHAT SALLY WAS HOPING FOR! TO GET THE SHE-DEMON BEFORE THE MIRROR!! WHERE SALLY COULD HURL THE FULL CONCENTRATION OF HER WILL... THE VERY FORCE OF HER ENTIRE BEING... IN AN ATTEMPT TO TRAP THE WILL OF HER ADVERSARY!
WHAT ARE YOU DOING? NO! NO! I WON'T LET YOU!

IT WAS A SILENT-- TERRIBLE STRUGGLE FOR DOMINATION! SALLY FOUGHT WITH EVERY OUNCE OF HER WILL POWER! SOMETHING EVIL AND DARK SCREAMED IN HER BRAIN! SALLY FELT HERSELF LURCH OUTWARD-- AND FOUND HERSELF ON THE FLOOR OF HER ROOM!

THE VOICE OF HER IMAGE STILL CLAMORED AND SHOUTED VILE OATHS IN SALLY'S MIND-- SALLY MEANT TO STILL IT FOREVER! HER FINGERS CURLED ABOUT THE HEAVY CANDLE- STICK ON HER VANITY!
SCREAM, YOU DEVIL! SCREAM ALL YOU WANT TO! BUT YOU'LL NEVER IMPRISON ME AGAIN! NEVER! NEVER!

THE SCREAMS WERE SUDDENLY LOST IN THE LOUD CRASH OF BREAKING GLASS! THE MIRROR AND ITS EVIL OCCUPANT WERE NO MORE!
CRASH!

SALLY! WHAT HAPPENED? I HEARD A SOUND LIKE THE BREAKING OF GLASS!
IT WAS MY MIRROR! I ACCIDENTALLY SMASHED IT!

BLAST THE MIRROR! AS LONG AS YOU'RE NOT HURT, I'M NOT WORRIED ABOUT IT! YOU CAN ALWAYS BUY A NEW ONE!

AND THAT'S WHAT SALLY DID. SHE BOUGHT A NEW MIRROR OF STANDARD MAKE-- MANUFACTURED WITHOUT BENEFIT OF LEGEND OR SPELL-- AND GUARANTEEING A WELL- BEHAVED IMAGE WHICH WAS CONTENT TO JUST IMITATE THE MOVE- MENTS OF ITS LIVING MODEL!

THE ADVENTURES OF PENROD

BY BOOTH TARKINGTON

CHAPTER XV
THE TWO FAMILIES

PENROD ENTERED THE SCHOOLROOM, Monday picturesquely leaning upon a man's cane shortened to support a cripple approaching the age of twelve. He arrived about twenty minutes late, limping deeply, his brave young mouth drawn with pain, and the sensation he created must have been a solace to him; the only possible criticism of this entrance being that it was just a shade too heroic. Perhaps for that reason it failed to stagger Miss Spence, a woman so saturated with suspicion that she penalized Penrod for tardiness as promptly and as coldly as if he had been a mere, ordinary, unmutilated boy. Nor would she entertain any discussion of the justice of her ruling. It seemed, almost, that she feared to argue with him.

However, the distinction of cane and limp remained to him, consolations which he protracted far into the week—until Thursday evening, in fact, when Mr. Schofield, observing from a window his son's pursuit of Duke round and round the backyard, confiscated the cane, with the promise that it should not remain idle if he saw Penrod limping again. Thus, succeeding a depressing Friday, another Saturday brought the necessity for new inventions.

It was a scented morning in apple-blossom time. At about ten of the clock Penrod emerged hastily from the kitchen door. His pockets bulged abnormally; so did his checks, and he swallowed with difficulty. A threatening mop, wielded by a cooklike arm in a checkered sleeve, followed him through the doorway, and he was preceded by a small, hurried, wistful dog with a warm doughnut in his mouth. The kitchen door slammed petulantly, enclosing the sore voice of Della, whereupon Penrod and Duke seated themselves upon the pleasant sward and immediately consumed the spoils of their raid.

From the cross-street which formed the side boundary of the Schofields' ample yard came a jingle of harness and the cadenced clatter of a pair of trotting horses, and Penrod, looking up, beheld the passing of a fat acquaintance, torpid amid the conservative splendours of a rather old-fashioned victoria. This was Roderick Magsworth Bitts, Junior, a fellow sufferer at the Friday Afternoon Dancing Class, but otherwise not often a companion: a home-sheltered lad, tutored privately and preserved against the coarsening influences of rude comradeship and miscellaneous information. Heavily overgrown in all physical dimensions, virtuous, and placid, this cloistered mutton was wholly uninteresting to Penrod Schofield. Nevertheless, Roderick Magsworth Bitts, Junior, was a personage on account of the importance of the Magsworth Bitts family; and it was Penrod's destiny to increase Roderick's

celebrity far, far beyond its present aristocratic limitations.

The Magsworth Bittses were important because they were impressive; there was no other reason. And they were impressive because they believed themselves important. The adults of the family were impregnably formal; they dressed with reticent elegance, and wore the same nose and the same expression—an expression which indicated that they knew something exquisite and sacred which other people could never know. Other people, in their presence, were apt to feel mysteriously ignoble and to become secretly uneasy about ancestors, gloves, and pronunciation. The Magsworth Bitts manner was withholding and reserved, though sometimes gracious, granting small smiles as great favours and giving off a chilling kind of preciousness. Naturally, when any citizen of the community did anything unconventional or improper, or made a mistake, or had a relative who went wrong, that citizen's first and worst fear was that the Magsworth Bittses would hear of it. In fact, this painful family had for years terrorized the community, though the community had never realized that it was terrorized, and invariably spoke of the family as the "most charming circle in town." By common consent, Mrs. Roderick Magsworth Bitts officiated as the supreme model as well as critic-in-chief of morals and deportment for all the unlucky people prosperous enough to be elevated to her acquaintance.

Magsworth was the important part of the name. Mrs. Roderick Magsworth Bitts was a Magsworth born, herself, and the Magsworth crest decorated not only Mrs. Magsworth Bitts' note-paper but was on the china, on the table linen, on the chimney-pieces, on the opaque glass of the front door, on the victoria, and on the harness, though omitted from the garden-hose and the lawn-mower.

Naturally, no sensible person dreamed of connecting that illustrious crest with the unfortunate and notorious Rena Magsworth whose name had grown week by week into larger and larger type upon the front pages of newspapers, owing to the gradually increasing public and official belief that she had poisoned a family of eight. However, the statement that no sensible person could have connected the Magsworth Bitts family with the arsenical Rena takes no account of Penrod Schofield.

Penrod never missed a murder, a hanging or an electrocution in the newspapers; he knew almost as much about Rena Magsworth as her jurymen did, though they sat in a court-room two hundred miles away, and he had it in mind—so frank he was—to ask Roderick Magsworth Bitts, Junior, if the murderess happened to be a relative.

The present encounter, being merely one of apathetic greeting, did not afford the opportunity. Penrod took off his cap, and Roderick, seated between his mother and one of his grown-up sisters, nodded sluggishly, but neither Mrs. Magsworth Bitts nor her daughter acknowledged the salutation of the boy in the yard. They disapproved of him as a person of little consequence, and that little, bad. Snubbed, Penrod thoughtfully restored his cap to his head. A boy can be cut as effectually as a man, and this one was chilled to a low temperature. He wondered if they despised him because they had seen a last fragment of doughnut in his hand; then he thought that perhaps it was Duke who had disgraced him. Duke was certainly no fashionable looking dog.

The resilient spirits of youth, however, presently revived, and discovering a spider upon one knee and a beetle simultaneously upon the other, Penrod forgot Mrs. Roderick Magsworth Bitts in the course of some experiments infringing upon the domain of Doctor Carrel. Penrod's efforts—with the aid of a pin—to effect a transference of living organism were unsuccessful; but he convinced himself forever that a spider cannot walk with a beetle's legs. Della then enhanced zoological interest by depositing upon the back porch a large rat-trap from the cellar, the prison of four live rats awaiting execution.

Penrod at once took possession, retiring to the empty stable, where he installed the rats in a small wooden box with a sheet of broken window-glass—held down by a brickbat—over the top. Thus the symptoms of their agitation, when the box was shaken or hammered upon, could be studied at leisure. Altogether this Saturday was starting splendidly.

After a time, the student's attention was withdrawn from his specimens by a peculiar smell, which, being followed up by a system of selective sniffing, proved to be an emanation leaking into the stable from the alley. He opened the back door.

Across the alley was a cottage which a thrifty neighbour had built on the rear line of his lot and rented to negroes; and the fact that a negro family was now in process of "moving in" was manifested by the presence of a thin mule and a ramshackle wagon, the latter laden with the semblance of a stove and a few other unpretentious household articles.

A very small darky boy stood near the mule. In his hand was a rusty chain, and at the end of the chain the delighted Penrod perceived the source of the special smell he was tracing—a large raccoon. Duke, who had shown not the slightest interest in the rats, set up a frantic barking and simulated a ravening assault upon the strange animal. It was only a bit of acting, however, for Duke was an old dog, had suffered much, and desired no unnecessary sorrow, wherefore he confined his demonstrations to alarums and excursions, and presently sat down at a distance and expressed himself by intermittent threatenings in a quavering falsetto.

"What's that 'coon's name?" asked Penrod, intending no discourtesy.

"Aim gommo mame," said the small darky.

"What?"

"Aim gommo mame."

"WHAT?"

The small darky looked annoyed.

"Aim GOMMO mame, I hell you," he said impatiently.

Penrod conceived that insult was intended.

"What's the matter of you?" he demanded advancing. "You get fresh with ME, and I'll—"

"Hyuh, white boy!" A coloured youth of Penrod's own age appeared in the doorway of the cottage. "You let 'at brothuh mine alone. He ain' do nothin' to you."

"Well, why can't he answer?"

"He can't. He can't talk no better'n what he WAS talkin'. He tongue-tie'."

"Oh," said Penrod, mollified. Then, obeying an impulse so universally aroused in the human breast under like circumstances that it has become a quip, he turned to the afflicted one.

"Talk some more," he begged eagerly.

"I hoe you ackoom aim gommo mame," was the prompt response, in which a slight ostentation was manifest. Unmistakable tokens of vanity had appeared upon the small, swart countenance.

"What's he mean?" asked Penrod, enchanted.

"He say he tole you 'at 'coon ain' got no name."

"What's YOUR name?"

"I'm name Herman."

"What's his name?" Penrod pointed to the tongue-tied boy.

"Verman."

"What!"

"Verman. Was three us boys in ow fam'ly. Ol'est one name Sherman. 'N'en come me; I'm Herman. 'N'en come him; he Verman. Sherman dead. Verman, he de littles' one."

"You goin' to live here?"

"Umhuh. Done move in f'm way outen on a fahm."

He pointed to the north with his right hand, and Penrod's eyes opened wide as they followed the gesture. Herman had no forefinger on that hand.

"Look there!" exclaimed Penrod. "You haven't got any finger!"

"*I* mum map," said Verman, with egregious pride.

"HE done 'at," interpreted Herman, chuckling. "Yessuh; done chop 'er spang off, long 'go. He's a playin' wif a ax an' I lay my finguh on de do'-sill an' I say, 'Verman, chop 'er off!' So Verman he chop 'er right spang off up to de roots! Yessuh."

"What FOR?"

"Jes' fo' nothin'."

"He hoe me hoo," remarked Verman.

"Yessuh, I tole him to," said Herman, "an' he chop 'er off, an' ey ain't airy oth' one evuh grown on wheres de ole one use to grow. Nosuh!"

"But what'd you tell him to do it for?"

"Nothin'. I 'es' said it 'at way—an' he jes' chop er off!"

Both brothers looked pleased and proud. Penrod's profound interest was flatteringly visible, a tribute to their unusualness.

"Hem bow goy," suggested Verman eagerly.

"Aw ri'," said Herman. "Ow sistuh Queenie, she a growed-up woman; she got a goituh."

"Got a what?"

"Goituh. Swellin' on her neck—grea' big swellin'. She heppin' mammy move in now. You look in de front-room winduh wheres she sweepin'; you kin see it on her."

Penrod looked in the window and was rewarded by a fine view of Queenie's goitre. He had never before seen one, and only

the lure of further conversation on the part of Verman brought him from the window.

"Verman say tell you 'bout pappy," explained Herman. "Mammy an' Queenie move in town an' go git de house all fix up befo' pappy git out."

"Out of where?"

"Jail. Pappy cut a man, an' de police done kep' him in jail evuh sense Chris'mus-time; but dey goin' tuhn him loose ag'in nex' week."

"What'd he cut the other man with?"

"Wif a pitchfawk."

Penrod began to feel that a lifetime spent with this fascinating family were all too short. The brothers, glowing with amiability, were as enraptured as he. For the first time in their lives they moved in the rich glamour of sensationalism. Herman was prodigal of gesture with his right hand; and Verman, chuckling with delight, talked fluently, though somewhat consciously. They cheerfully agreed to keep the raccoon—already beginning to be mentioned as "our ,coon" by Penrod—in Mr. Schofield's empty stable, and, when the animal had been chained to the wall near the box of rats and supplied with a pan of fair water, they assented to their new friend's suggestion (inspired by a fine sense of the artistic harmonies) that the heretofore nameless pet be christened Sherman, in honour of their deceased relative.

At this juncture was heard from the front yard the sound of that yodelling which is the peculiar accomplishment of those whose voices have not "changed." Penrod yodelled a response; and Mr. Samuel Williams appeared, a large bundle under his arm.

"Yay, Penrod!" was his greeting, casual enough from without; but, having entered, he stopped short and emitted a prodigious whistle. "YA-A-AY!" he then shouted. "Look at the 'coon!"

"I guess you better say, 'Look at the 'coon!'" Penrod returned proudly. "They's a good deal more'n him to look at, too. Talk some, Verman." Verman complied.

Sam was warmly interested. "What'd you say his name was?" he asked.

"Verman."

"How d'you spell it?"

"V-e-r-m-a-n," replied Penrod, having previously received this information from Herman.

"Oh!" said Sam.

"Point to sumpthing, Herman," Penrod commanded, and Sam's excitement, when Herman pointed was sufficient to the occasion.

Penrod, the discoverer, continued his exploitation of the manifold wonders of the Sherman, Herman, and Verman collection. With the air of a proprietor he escorted Sam into the alley for a good look at Queenie (who seemed not to care for her increasing celebrity) and proceeded to a dramatic climax—the recital of the episode of the pitchfork and its consequences.

The cumulative effect was enormous, and could have but one possible result. The normal boy is always at least one half Barnum.

"Let's get up a SHOW!"

Penrod and Sam both claimed to have said it first, a question left unsettled in the ecstasies of hurried preparation. The bundle under Sam's arm, brought with no definite purpose, proved to have been an inspiration. It consisted of broad sheets of light yellow wrapping-paper, discarded by Sam's mother in her spring house-cleaning. There were half-filled cans and buckets of paint in the storeroom adjoining the carriage-house, and presently the side wall of the stable flamed information upon the passer-by from a great and spreading poster.

"Publicity," primal requisite of all theatrical and amphitheatrical enterprise thus provided, subsequent arrangements proceeded with a fury of energy which transformed the empty hayloft. True, it is impossible to say just what the hay-loft was transformed into, but history warrantably clings to the statement that it was transformed. Duke and Sherman were secured to the rear wall at a considerable distance from each other, after an exhibition of reluctance on the part of Duke, during which he displayed a nervous energy and agility almost miraculous in so small and middle-aged a dog. Benches were improvised for spectators; the rats were brought up; finally the rafters, corn-crib, and hay-chute were ornamented with flags and strips of bunting from Sam Williams' attic, Sam returning from the excursion wearing an old silk hat, and accompanied (on account of a rope) by a fine dachshund encountered on the highway. In the matter of personal decoration paint was generously used: an interpretation of the spiral, inclining to whites and greens, becoming brilliantly effective upon the dark facial backgrounds of Herman and Verman; while the countenances of Sam and Penrod were each supplied with the black moustache and imperial, lacking which, no professional showman can be esteemed conscientious.

It was regretfully decided, in council, that no attempt be made to add Queenie to the list of exhibits, her brothers warmly declining to act as ambassadors in that cause. They were certain Queenie would not like the idea, they said, and Herman picturesquely described her activity on occasions when she had been annoyed by too much attention to her appearance. However, Penrod's disappointment was alleviated by an inspiration which came to him in a moment of pondering upon the dachshund, and the entire party went forth to add an enriching line to the poster.

They found a group of seven, including two adults, already gathered in the street to read and admire this work.

SCHoFiELD & WiLLiAMS
BiG SHOW
ADMiSSioN 1 CENT oR 20 PiNS

MUSUEM oF CURioSiTES
Now GoiNG oN

SHERMAN HERMAN & VERMAN
THiER FATHERS iN JAiL
STABED A MAN WiTH A
PiTCHFORK

SHERMAN THE WiLD ANIMAL
CAPTURED iN AFRiCA

HERMAN THE ONE FiNGERED
TATOOD WILD MAN
VERMAN THE SAVAGE TATOOD
WILD BoY TALKS ONLY iN HiS
NAiTiVE
LANGUAGS.

Do NoT FAIL TO SEE DUKE
THE INDiAN DOG

ALSO THE MiCHiGAN
TRAiNED RATS

A heated argument took place between Sam and Penrod, the point at issue being settled, finally, by the drawing of straws; whereupon Penrod, with pardonable self-importance—in the presence of an audience now increased to nine—slowly painted the words inspired by the dachshund:

IMPoRTENT Do NoT MISS
THE SoUTH
AMERiCAN DoG
PART ALLIGATOR.

CHAPTER XVI
THE NEW STAR

Sam, Penrod, Herman, and Verman withdrew in considerable state from non-paying view, and, repairing to the hay-loft, declared the exhibition open to the public. Oral proclamation was made by Sam, and then the loitering multitude was enticed by the seductive strains of a band; the two partners performing upon combs and paper, Herman and Verman upon tin pans with sticks.

The effect was immediate. Visitors appeared upon the stairway and sought admission. Herman and Verman took position among the exhibits, near the wall; Sam stood at the entrance, officiating as barker and ticket-seller; while Penrod, with debonair suavity, acted as curator, master of ceremonies, and lecturer. He greeted the first to enter with a courtly bow. They consisted of Miss Rennsdale and her nursery governess, and they paid spot cash for their admission.

"Walk in, lay-deeze, walk right in—pray do not obstruck the passage-way," said Penrod, in a remarkable voice. "Pray be seated; there is room for each and all."

Miss Rennsdale and governess were followed by Mr. Georgie Bassett and baby sister (which proves the perfection of Georgie's character) and six or seven other neighbourhood children—a most satisfactory audience, although, subsequent to Miss Rennsdale and governess, admission was wholly by pin.

"GEN-til-mun and LAY-deeze," shouted Penrod, "I will first call your at-tain-shon to our genuine South American dog, part alligator!" He pointed to the dachshund, and added, in his ordinary tone, "That's him." Straightway reassuming the character of showman, he bellowed: "NEXT, you see Duke, the genuine, full-blooded Indian dog from the far Western Plains and Rocky Mountains. NEXT, the trained Michigan rats, captured way up there, and trained to jump and run all around the box at the—at the—at the slightest PRE-text!" He paused, partly to take breath and partly to enjoy his own surprised discovery that this phrase was in his vocabulary.

"At the slightest PRE-text!" he repeated, and continued, suiting the action to the word: "I will now hammer upon the box and each and all may see these genuine full-blooded Michigan rats perform at the slightest PRE-text! There! (That's all they do now, but I and Sam are goin' to train 'em lots more before this afternoon.) GEN-til-mun and LAY-deeze I will kindly now call your at-tain-shon to Sherman, the wild animal from Africa, costing the lives of the wild trapper and many of his companions. NEXT, let me kindly interodoos Herman and Ver-man. Their father got mad and stuck his pitchfork right inside of another man, exactly as promised upon the advertise-ments outside the big tent, and got put in jail. Look at them well, gen-til-mun and lay-deeze, there is no extra charge, and RE-MEM-BUR you are each and all now looking at two wild, tattooed men which the father of is in jail. Point, Her-man. Each and all will have a chance to see. Point to sumpthing else, Herman. This is the only genuine one-fingered tat-tooed wild man. Last on the programme, gen-til-mun and lay-deeze, we have Ver-man, the savage tattooed wild boy, that can't speak only his native foreign lan-guages. Talk some, Verman."

Verman obliged and made an instan-taneous hit. He was encored rapturously, again and again; and, thrilling with the unique pleasure of being appreciated and misunderstood at the same time, would have talked all day but too gladly. Sam Williams, however, with a true showman's

foresight, whispered to Penrod, who rang down on the monologue.

"GEN-til-mun and LAY-deeze, this closes our pufformance. Pray pass out quietly and with as little jostling as possi-ble. As soon as you are all out there's goin' to be a new pufformance, and each and all are welcome at the same and simple price of admission. Pray pass out qui-etly and with as little jostling as possible. RE-MEM-BUR the price is only one cent, the tenth part of a dime, or twenty pins, no bent ones taken. Pray pass out quietly and with as little jostling as possi-ble. The Schofield and Williams Military Band will play before each pufformance, and each and all are welcome for the same and simple price of admission. Pray pass out quietly and with as little jostling as possible."

Forthwith, the Schofield and Wil-liams Military Band began a second over-ture, in which something vaguely like a tune was at times distinguishable; and all of the first audience returned, most of them having occupied the interval in hasty excursions for more pins; Miss Rennsdale and governess, however, again paying coin of the Republic and receiving deference and the best seats accordingly. And when a third performance found all of the same inveterate patrons once more crowding the auditorium, and seven recruits added, the pleasurable excite-ment of the partners in their venture will be understood by any one who has seen a metropolitan manager strolling about the foyer of his theatre some evening during the earlier stages of an assured "phenom-enal run."

From the first, there was no ques-tion which feature of the entertain-ment was the attraction extraordinary: Verman—Verman, the savage tattooed wild boy, speaking only his native for-eign languages—Verman was a triumph! Beaming, wreathed in smiles, melodious, incredibly fluent, he had but to open his lips and a dead hush fell upon the audience. Breathless, they leaned forward, hanging upon his every semi-syllable, and, when Penrod checked the flow, burst into thunders of applause, which Verman received with happy laughter.

Alas! he delayed not o'er long to display all the egregiousness of a new star; but for a time there was no caprice of his too eccentric to be forgiven. During Penrod's lecture upon the other curios, the tattooed wild boy continually stamped his foot, grinned, and gesticulated, tapping his tiny chest, and pointing to himself as it were to say: "Wait for Me! I am the Big Show." So soon they learn; so soon they learn! And (again alas!) this spoiled darling of public favour, like many another, was fated to know, in good time, the fickleness of that favour.

But during all the morning performances he was the idol of his audience and looked it! The climax of his popularity came during the fifth overture of the Schofield and Williams Military Band, when the music was quite drowned in the agitated clamours of Miss Rennsdale, who was endeavouring to ascend the stairs in spite of the physical dissuasion of her governess.

"I WON'T go home to lunch!" screamed Miss Rennsdale, her voice accompanied by a sound of ripping. "I WILL hear the tattooed wild boy talk some more! It's lovely—I WILL hear him talk! I WILL! I WILL! I want to listen to Verman—I WANT to—I WANT to—"

Wailing, she was borne away—of her sex not the first to be fascinated by obscurity, nor the last to champion its eloquence.

Verman was almost unendurable after this, but, like many, many other managers, Schofield and Williams restrained their choler, and even laughed fulsomely when their principal attraction essayed the role of a comedian in private, and capered and squawked in sheer, fatuous vanity.

The first performance of the afternoon rivalled the successes of the morning, and although Miss Rennsdale was detained at home, thus drying up the single source of cash income developed before lunch, Maurice Levy appeared, escorting Marjorie Jones, and paid coin for two admissions, dropping the money into Sam's hand with a careless—nay, a contemptuous—gesture. At sight of Marjorie, Penrod Schofield flushed under his new moustache (repainted since noon) and lectured as he had never lectured before. A new grace invested his every gesture; a new sonorousness rang in his voice; a simple and manly pomposity marked his very walk as he passed from curio to curio. And when he fearlessly handled the box of rats and hammered upon it with cool insouciance, he beheld—for the first time in his life—a purl of admiration eddying in Marjorie's lovely eye, a certain softening of that eye. And then Verman spake and Penrod was forgotten. Marjorie's eye rested upon him no more.

A heavily equipped chauffeur ascended the stairway, bearing the message that Mrs. Levy awaited her son and his lady. Thereupon, having devoured the last sound permitted (by the managers) to issue from Verman, Mr. Levy and Miss Jones departed to a real matinee at a real theatre, the limpid eyes of Marjorie looking back softly over her shoulder—but only at the tattooed wild boy. Nearly always it is woman who puts the irony into life.

After this, perhaps because of sated curiosity, perhaps on account of a pin famine, the attendance began to languish. Only four responded to the next call of the band; the four dwindled to three; finally the entertainment was given for one blase auditor, and Schofield and

Williams looked depressed. Then followed an interval when the band played in vain.

About three o'clock Schofield and Williams were gloomily discussing various unpromising devices for startling the public into a renewal of interest, when another patron unexpectedly appeared and paid a cent for his admission. News of the Big Show and Museum of Curiosities had at last penetrated the far, cold spaces of interstellar niceness, for this new patron consisted of no less than Roderick Magsworth Bitts, Junior, escaped in a white "sailor suit" from the Manor during a period of severe maternal and tutorial preoccupation.

He seated himself without parley, and the pufformance was offered for his entertainment with admirable conscientiousness. True to the Lady Clara caste and training, Roderick's pale, fat face expressed nothing except an impervious superiority and, as he sat, cold and unimpressed upon the front bench, like a large, white lump, it must be said that he made a discouraging audience "to play to." He was not, however, unresponsive—far from it. He offered comment very chilling to the warm grandiloquence of the orator.

"That's my uncle Ethelbert's dachshund," he remarked, at the beginning of the lecture. "You better take him back if you don't want to get arrested." And when Penrod, rather uneasily ignoring the interruption, proceeded to the exploitation of the genuine, full-blooded Indian dog, Duke, "Why don't you try to give that old dog away?" asked Roderick. "You couldn't sell him."

"My papa would buy me a lots better 'coon than that," was the information volunteered a little later, "only I wouldn't want the nasty old thing."

Herman of the missing finger obtained no greater indulgence. "Pooh!"

said Roderick. "We have two fox-terriers in our stables that took prizes at the kennel show, and their tails were BIT off. There's a man that always bites fox-terriers' tails off."

"Oh, my gosh, what a lie!" exclaimed Sam Williams ignorantly.

"Go on with the show whether he likes it or not, Penrod. He's paid his money."

Verman, confident in his own singular powers, chuckled openly at the failure of the other attractions to charm the frosty visitor, and, when his turn came, poured forth a torrent of conversation which was straightway damned.

"Rotten," said Mr. Bitts languidly. "Anybody could talk like that. *I* could do it if I wanted to."

Verman paused suddenly.

"YES, you could!" exclaimed Penrod, stung. "Let's hear you do it, then."

"Yessir!" the other partner shouted. "Let's just hear you DO it!"

"I said I could if I wanted to," responded Roderick. "I didn't say I WOULD."

"Yay! Knows he can't!" sneered Sam.

"I can, too, if I try."

"Well, let's hear you try!"

So challenged, the visitor did try, but, in the absence of an impartial jury, his effort was considered so pronounced a failure that he was howled down, derided, and mocked with great clamours.

"Anyway," said Roderick, when things had quieted down, "if I couldn't get up a better show than this I'd sell out and leave town."

Not having enough presence of mind to inquire what he would sell out, his adversaries replied with mere formless yells of scorn.

"I could get up a better show than this with my left hand," Roderick asserted.

"Well, what would you have in your ole show?" asked Penrod, condescending to language.

"That's all right, what I'd HAVE. I'd have enough!"

"You couldn't get Herman and Verman in your ole show."

"No, and I wouldn't want 'em, either!"

"Well, what WOULD you have?" insisted Penrod derisively. "You'd have to have SUMPTHING—you couldn't be a show yourself!"

"How do YOU know?" This was but meandering while waiting for ideas, and evoked another yell.

"You think you could be a show all by yourself?" demanded Penrod.

"How do YOU know I couldn't?"

Two white boys and two black boys shrieked their scorn of the boaster.

"I could, too!" Roderick raised his voice to a sudden howl, obtaining a hearing.

"Well, why don't you tell us how?"

"Well, *I* know HOW, all right," said Roderick. "If anybody asks you, you can just tell him I know HOW, all right."

"Why, you can't DO anything," Sam began argumentatively. "You talk about being a show all by yourself; what could you try to do? Show us sumpthing you can do."

"I didn't say I was going to DO anything," returned the badgered one, still evading.

"Well, then, how'd you BE a show?" Penrod demanded. "WE got a show here, even if Herman didn't point or Verman didn't talk. Their father stabbed a man with a pitchfork, I guess, didn't he?"

"How do *I* know?"

"Well, I guess he's in jail, ain't he?"

"Well, what if their father is in jail? I didn't say he wasn't, did I?"

"Well, YOUR father ain't in jail, is he?"

"Well, I never said he was, did I?"

"Well, then," continued Penrod, "how could you be a—" He stopped abruptly, staring at Roderick, the birth of an idea plainly visible in his altered expression. He had suddenly remembered his intention to ask Roderick Magsworth Bitts, Junior, about Rena Magsworth, and this recollection collided in his mind with the irritation produced by Roderick's claiming some mysterious attainment which would warrant his setting up as a show in his single person. Penrod's whole manner changed instantly.

"Roddy," he asked, almost overwhelmed by a prescience of something vast and magnificent, "Roddy, are you any relation of Rena Magsworth?"

Roderick had never heard of Rena Magsworth, although a concentration of the sentence yesterday pronounced upon her had burned, black and horrific, upon the face of every newspaper in the country. He was not allowed to read the journals of the day and his family's indignation over the sacrilegious coincidence of the name had not been expressed in his presence. But he saw that it was an awesome name to Penrod Schofield and Samuel Williams. Even Herman and Verman, though lacking many educational advantages on account of a long residence in the country, were informed on the subject of Rena Magsworth through hearsay, and they joined in the portentous silence.

"Roddy," repeated Penrod, "honest, is Rena Magsworth some relation of yours?"

There is no obsession more dangerous to its victims than a conviction especially an inherited one—of superiority: this world is so full of Missourians. And from his earliest years Roderick Magsworth Bitts, Junior, had been trained to believe in the importance of the Magsworth family. At every meal he absorbed a sense of Magsworth greatness, and yet, in his infrequent meetings with persons

of his own age and sex, he was treated as negligible. Now, dimly, he perceived that there was a Magsworth claim of some sort which was impressive, even to boys. Magsworth blood was the essential of all true distinction in the world, he knew. Consequently, having been driven into a cul-de-sac, as a result of flagrant and unfounded boasting, he was ready to take advantage of what appeared to be a triumphal way out.

"Roddy," said Penrod again, with solemnity, "is Rena Magsworth some relation of yours?"

"IS she, Roddy?" asked Sam, almost hoarsely.

"She's my aunt!" shouted Roddy.

Silence followed. Sam and Penrod, spellbound, gazed upon Roderick Magsworth Bitts, Junior. So did Herman and Verman. Roddy's staggering lie had changed the face of things utterly. No one questioned it; no one realized that it was much too good to be true.

"Roddy," said Penrod, in a voice tremulous with hope, "Roddy, will you join our show?"

Roddy joined.

Even he could see that the offer implied his being starred as the paramount attraction of a new order of things. It was obvious that he had swelled out suddenly, in the estimation of the other boys, to that importance which he had been taught to believe his native gift and natural right. The sensation was pleasant. He had often been treated with effusion by grown-up callers and by acquaintances of his mothers and sisters; he had heard ladies speak of him as "charming" and "that delightful child," and little girls had sometimes shown him deference, but until this moment no boy had ever allowed him, for one moment, to presume even to equality. Now, in a trice, he was not only admitted to comradeship, but patently valued as something rare and sacred to be acclaimed and pedestalled. In fact, the very first thing that Schofield and Williams did was to find a box for him to stand upon.

The misgivings roused in Roderick's bosom by the subsequent activities of the firm were not bothersome enough to make him forego his prominence as Exhibit A. He was not a "quick-minded" boy, and it was long (and much happened) before he thoroughly comprehended the causes of his new celebrity. He had a shadowy feeling that if the affair came to be heard of at home it might not be liked, but, intoxicated by the glamour and bustle which surround a public character, he made no protest. On the contrary, he entered whole-heartedly into the preparations for the new show. Assuming, with Sam's assistance, a blue moustache and "side-burns," he helped in the painting of a new poster, which, supplanting the old one on the wall of the stable facing the cross-street, screamed bloody murder at the passers in that rather populous thoroughfare.

SCHoFiELD & WiLLiAMS
NEW BIG SHoW

RoDERiCK MAGSWoRTH BiTTS JR
ONLY LiViNG NEPHEW oF
RENA MAGSWORTH
THE FAMOS MUDERESS

GoiNG To BE HUNG
NEXT JULY
KiLED EiGHT PEOPLE
PUT ARSiNECK iN THiER MiLK

ALSO
SHERMAN HERMAN
AND VERMAN

THE MiCHiGAN RATS DOG PART
ALLiGATOR
DUKE THE GENUiNE
InDiAN DoG

ADMISSioN 1 CENT oR
20 PINS SAME AS BEFORE

Do NoT
MISS THIS CHANSE TO SEE
RoDERICK
ONLY LiViNG NEPHEW
oF RENA MAGSWORTH
THE GREAT FAMOS
MUDERESS

GoiNG To BE
HUNG

CHAPTER XVII
RETIRING FROM
THE SHOW
BUSINESS

Megaphones were constructed out of heavy wrapping-paper, and Penrod, Sam, and Herman set out in different directions, delivering vocally the inflammatory proclamation of the poster to a large section of the residential quarter, and leaving Roderick Magsworth Bitts, Junior, with Verman in the loft, shielded from all deadhead eyes. Upon the return of the heralds, the Schofield and Williams Military Band played deafeningly, and an awakened public once more thronged to fill the coffers of the firm.

Prosperity smiled again. The very first audience after the acquisition of Roderick was larger than the largest of the morning. Master Bitts—the only exhibit placed upon a box—was a supercurio. All eyes fastened upon him and remained, hungrily feasting, throughout Penrod's luminous oration.

But the glory of one light must ever be the dimming of another. We dwell in a vale of seesaws—and cobwebs spin fastest upon laurel. Verman, the tattooed wild boy, speaking only in his native foreign languages, Verman the gay, Verman the caperer, capered no more; he chuckled no more, he beckoned no more, nor tapped his chest, nor wreathed his idolatrous face in smiles. Gone, all gone, were his little artifices for attracting the general attention to himself; gone was every engaging mannerism which had endeared him to the mercurial public. He squatted against the wall and glowered at the new sensation. It was the old story—the old, old story of too much temperament: Verman was suffering from artistic jealousy.

The second audience contained a cash-paying adult, a spectacled young man whose poignant attention was very flattering. He remained after the lecture, and put a few questions to Roddy, which were answered rather confusedly upon promptings from Penrod. The young man went away without having stated the object of his interrogations, but it became quite plain, later in the day. This same object caused the spectacled young man to make several brief but stimulating calls directly after leaving the Schofield and Williams Big Show, and the consequences thereof loitered not by the wayside.

The Big Show was at high tide. Not only was the auditorium filled and throbbing; there was an indubitable line—by no means wholly juvenile—waiting for admission to the next pufformance. A group stood in the street examining the poster earnestly as it glowed in the long, slanting rays of the westward sun, and people in automobiles and other vehicles had halted wheel in the street to read the message so piquantly given to the world. These were the conditions when a crested victoria arrived at a gallop, and a large, chastely magnificent and highly flushed woman descended, and progressed across the yard with an air of violence.

At sight of her, the adults of the waiting line hastily disappeared, and most of the pausing vehicles moved instantly on

their way. She was followed by a stricken man in livery.

The stairs to the auditorium were narrow and steep; Mrs. Roderick Magsworth Bitts was of a stout favour; and the voice of Penrod was audible during the ascent.

"RE-MEM-BUR, gentilmun and lay-deeze, each and all are now gazing upon Roderick Magsworth Bitts, Junior, the only living nephew of the great Rena Magsworth. She stuck ars'nic in the milk of eight separate and distinck people to put in their coffee and each and all of 'em died. The great ars'nic murderess, Rena Magsworth, gentilmun and lay-deeze, and Roddy's her only living nephew. She's a relation of all the Bitts family, but he's her one and only living nephew. RE-MEM-BUR! Next July she's goin' to be hung, and, each and all, you now see before you—"

Penrod paused abruptly, seeing something before himself—the august and awful presence which filled the entryway. And his words (it should be related) froze upon his lips.

Before HERSELF, Mrs. Roderick Magsworth Bitts saw her son—her scion—wearing a moustache and sideburns of blue, and perched upon a box flanked by Sherman and Verman, the Michigan rats, the Indian dog Duke, Herman, and the dog part alligator.

Roddy, also, saw something before himself. It needed no prophet to read the countenance of the dread apparition in the entryway. His mouth opened—remained open—then filled to capacity with a calamitous sound of grief not unmingled with apprehension.

Penrod's reason staggered under the crisis. For a horrible moment he saw Mrs. Roderick Magsworth Bitts approaching like some fatal mountain in avalanche. She seemed to grow larger and redder; lightnings played about her head; he had a vague consciousness of the audience spraying out in flight, of the squealings, tramplings and dispersals of a stricken field. The mountain was close upon him—

He stood by the open mouth of the hay-chute which went through the floor to the manger below. Penrod also went through the floor. He propelled himself into the chute and shot down, but not quite to the manger, for Mr. Samuel Williams had thoughtfully stepped into the chute a moment in advance of his partner. Penrod lit upon Sam.

Catastrophic noises resounded in the loft; volcanoes seemed to romp upon the stairway.

There ensued a period when only a shrill keening marked the passing of Roderick as he was borne to the tumbril. Then all was silence.

. . . Sunset, striking through a western window, rouged the walls of the Schofields' library, where gathered a joint family council and court martial of four—Mrs. Schofield, Mr. Schofield, and Mr. and Mrs. Williams, parents of Samuel of that ilk. Mr. Williams read aloud a conspicuous passage from the last edition of the evening paper:

"Prominent people here believed close relations of woman sentenced to hang. Angry denial by Mrs. R. Magsworth Bitts. Relationship admitted by younger member of family. His statement confirmed by boy-friends—"

"Don't!" said Mrs. Williams, addressing her husband vehemently. "We've all read it a dozen times. We've got plenty of trouble on our hands without hearing THAT again!"

Singularly enough, Mrs. Williams did not look troubled; she looked as if she were trying to look troubled. Mrs. Schofield wore a similar expression. So did Mr. Schofield. So did Mr. Williams.

"What did she say when she called YOU up?" Mrs. Schofield inquired breathlessly of Mrs. Williams.

"She could hardly speak at first, and then when she did talk, she talked so fast I couldn't understand most of it, and—"

"It was just the same when she tried to talk to me," said Mrs. Schofield, nodding.

"I never did hear any one in such a state before," continued Mrs. Williams. "So furious—"

"Quite justly, of course," said Mrs. Schofield.

"Of course. And she said Penrod and Sam had enticed Roderick away from home—usually he's not allowed to go outside the yard except with his tutor or a servant—and had told him to say that horrible creature was his aunt—"

"How in the world do you suppose Sam and Penrod ever thought of such a thing as THAT!" exclaimed Mrs. Schofield. "It must have been made up just for their 'show.' Della says there were just STREAMS going in and out all day. Of course it wouldn't have happened, but this was the day Margaret and I spend every month in the country with Aunt Sarah, and I didn't DREAM—"

"She said one thing I thought rather tactless," interrupted Mrs. Williams. "Of course we must allow for her being dreadfully excited and wrought up, but I do think it wasn't quite delicate in her, and she's usually the very soul of delicacy. She said that Roderick had NEVER been allowed to associate with—common boys—"

"Meaning Sam and Penrod," said Mrs. Schofield. "Yes, she said that to me, too."

"She said that the most awful thing about it," Mrs. Williams went on, "was that, though she's going to prosecute the newspapers, many people would always believe the story, and—"

"Yes, I imagine they will," said Mrs. Schofield musingly. "Of course you and I and everybody who really knows the Bitts and Magsworth families understand the perfect absurdity of it; but I suppose there are ever so many who'll believe it, no matter what the Bittses and Magsworths say."

"Hundreds and hundreds!" said Mrs. Williams. "I'm afraid it will be a great come-down for them."

"I'm afraid so," said Mrs. Schofield gently. "A very great one—yes, a very, very great one."

"Well," observed Mrs. Williams, after a thoughtful pause, "there's only one thing to be done, and I suppose it had better be done right away."

She glanced toward the two gentlemen.

"Certainly," Mr. Schofield agreed. "But where ARE they?"

"Have you looked in the stable?" asked his wife.

"I searched it. They've probably started for the far West."

"Did you look in the sawdust-box?"

"No, I didn't."

"Then that's where they are."

Thus, in the early twilight, the now historic stable was approached by two fathers charged to do the only thing to be done. They entered the storeroom.

"Penrod!" said Mr. Schofield.

"Sam!" said Mr. Williams.

Nothing disturbed the twilight hush.

But by means of a ladder, brought from the carriage-house, Mr. Schofield mounted to the top of the sawdust-box. He looked within, and discerned the dim outlines of three quiet figures, the third being that of a small dog.

The two boys rose, upon command, descended the ladder after Mr. Schofield, bringing Duke with them, and stood before the authors of their being, who bent upon them sinister and threatening brows. With hanging heads and despondent countenances, each still ornamented with a moustache and an imperial, Penrod and Sam awaited sentence.

This is a boy's lot: anything he does, anything whatever, may afterward turn out to have been a crime—he never knows.

And punishment and clemency are alike inexplicable.

Mr. Williams took his son by the ear.

"You march home!" he commanded.

Sam marched, not looking back, and his father followed the small figure implacably.

"You goin' to whip me?" quavered Penrod, alone with Justice.

"Wash your face at that hydrant," said his father sternly.

About fifteen minutes later, Penrod, hurriedly entering the corner drug store, two blocks distant, was astonished to perceive a familiar form at the soda counter.

"Yay, Penrod," said Sam Williams. "Want some sody? Come on. He didn't lick me. He didn't do anything to me at all. He gave me a quarter."

"So'd mine," said Penrod.

TO BE CONTINUED IN LITERARY OUTLAW #6

the GHOST RIDER

To an outlaw, who must live in shadow and fear, a good hideout is a very precious thing. Owlhoot Clasher thought his little hideaway was so safe that he could hide even from the Ghost Rider! But— his own trick tricks him when he sets "A TRAP FOR NEMESIS!"

AYERS

HAW-HAW-HEE-HAW! FOUR ROBBERIES IN TWO WEEKS AN' EVERY SINGLE ONE A SUCCESS! WE'RE MAKIN' A FORTUNE, MEN! AN' NOBODY BUT NOBODY - WILL EVER FIND OUT WHAR WE GOT THET HARD CASH STASHED AWAY!

RIGHT, CLASHER! WOW, WHUT A HIDEOUT WE GOT FER THET STUFF!

YUH'RE A SMART BOSS, CLASHER! AN' TOP O' EVERYTHIN' WE GOT A FOOLPROOF JOB LINED UP ON THIS TOWN BANK FER TOMORROW NIGHT

But!
NOTHIN' IS FOOLPROOF TO THE GHOST RIDER— HE WHO WALKS THE WAYS OF DARKNESS.

I AM WATCHING YOU, VILLAINS— I WILL THWART YOUR PLANS AND I WILL FIND YOUR HIDEOUT TOO!
THET'S THE GHOST RIDER! SHOOT 'IM! HE AIN'T NO GHOST AT ALL!

WHO TURNED OUT THUH LIGHTS?
YE-OW
BANG!
CRASH!
SOMEBODY HIT ME! WHY YUH VARMINT, I'LL—!
POW!

I GOT 'IM! TURN ON THUH LIGHTS!

WE GOT 'IM ALL RIGHT! NOW RIP OFF THET SHEET AN' LET'S SEE WHO HE IS!

IT'S ME, YUH DUMB SOAKS! THUH GHOST RIDER GOT CLEAN AWAY!

MEBBE HE JEST-GULP-VANISHED! MEBBE HE IS A GHOST! CLASHER, OLD BOY, OLD BOY— I'M SKEERED...!

BAH! THERE AIN'T NO SECH THING AS GHOSTS! FER A SPOOK, THET HOMBRE SHORE GOT A HARD FIST! THET JASPER KIN BE BEAT AN' WE'RE THUH ONES WHO KIN BEAT 'IM! I'LL SHOW YUH HOW TUH GIT RID OF THUH GHOST RIDER FER GOOD!
NEXT DAY, AT NOON...
KEEP A SHARP LOOKOUT, MEN. THUH GHOST RIDER DON'T RIDE EXCEPT AT NIGHT, BUT THAR'S NO USE TAKIN' CHANCES. WE'LL TRAP 'IM, ALL RIGHT.
BUT, BOSS— WE'RE HEADIN' RIGHT FER OUR HIDEOUT!
RIGHT! OUR HIDEOUT IS JEST AROUND THE BEND. BUT RIGHT AT THIS SPOT IS WHAR WE'RE GOIN' TUH TRAP THUH GHOST RIDER. MUSH, YOU GO UP ON THUH HILL AN' STAND LOOKOUT. WE'RE GOIN' TUH START DIGGIN' RIGHT HYAR!
WE'RE GOIN' TUH PULL THET JOB AT THUH BANK TONIGHT JEST LIKE WE PLANNED, SEE? AN' EF THUH GHOST RIDER INTERFERES...
I GET IT! WE HEAD FER THUH HIDEOUT AN' LET THUH HOMBRE CHASE US...
RIGHT! WE STEER AROUND THIS HOLE 'CAUSE WE KNOW ABOUT IT. BUT THE GHOST RIDER WILL FALL RIGHT IN! IT'S JEST LIKE A ELEPHANT TRAP LIKE THEY USE IN AFRICA.
HE'LL BREAK HIS NECK— I HOPE! SMART!
AN' EVEN EF HE DON'T BREAK HIS NECK, WE GOT HIM HELPLESS. WE KIN FINISH HIM OFF WITH OUR GUNS! OKAY, MEN— LET'S GIT BACK TUH TOWN AN' GIT READY FER THET JOB TONIGHT! I ALREADY GOT THUH KEY FER THE BACK DOOR...
THAT NIGHT— MIDNIGHT!
SURPRISED?
WHUT THUH—!
BANK

THIS'LL HOLD HIM! BUT PLUG HIM ANYWAY, JEST TUH MAKE SHORE! AN' MOVE FAST!

CAN YOU MOVE FASTER THAN THE GHOST RIDER? DROP YOUR GUN, VILE MAN!
HYAR HE IS — ALREADY!

DROP IT, I SAY! IF THIS NIGHTWATCHMAN IS HURT, IT WILL GO BADLY WITH YOU!
GIT, MEN — GIT!
C-R-A-A-N-G!

THE COWARDS RUN AWAY — WELL, LET THEM! I SHALL CATCH UP WITH THEM LATER. FIRST TO SEE ABOUT THE NIGHTWATCHMAN — AH, KNOCKED UNCONSCIOUS, BUT NOT SERIOUSLY HURT. NOW....!

...NOW TO HAVE A RECKONING WITH THESE NIGHTBIRDS OF EVIL!...
UP, SPECTRE! UP, WHITE HORSE!

HE'S CHASIN' US — GOOD! JEST LIKE WE PLANNED! REMEMBER TUH RIDE AROUND THET TRAP, MEN!
WE WILL! IT'S JEST AROUND THET BEND, NOW!

WHAT —!... EASY, SPECTRE!
HOORAY! IT WORKED!

COME ON, MEN~ HURRY! GIT YORE GUNS READY! WE'LL FINISH HIM OFF!
WE GOT 'IM NOW!

GULP! EMPTY!
QUICK! GIT THET LONG BRANCH AN' POKE DOWN IN THAR. HE'S GOT TO BE IN THAR— HE'S JEST GOT TUH...

I·DON'T·FEEL·A·THING! NOTHIN' AT ALL!

IN FACT— THAR JEST AIN'T NO BOTTOM! GULP! MEBBE - MEBBE THUH GHOST RIDER IS A G·G·GHOST!

HOOOOO-HOOOO
YOOOOO! MAKE FER THUH HIDEOUT, MEN! LET'S GIT!

QUICK! CAIN'T YOU MEN UNHINGE THET ROCK FASTER?

SAFE! SAFE— I THINK! QUICK, MEN— LET'S DIG UP OUR LOOT AN' OUR PROVISIONS! QUICK!

WE'LL MOVE THIS STUFF EVEN FARTHER BACK IN ONE OF THE TUNNELS OF THIS ABANDONED MINE. LET'S GO!

WE'LL BLOCK UP THET ENTRANCE TUH THIS SIDE TUNNEL! WE'LL SEAL IT FER DOUBLE PROTECTION! WE SHUT OURSELVES OFF COMPLETELY! WE GOT ENOUGH FOOD TUH STAY HERE FER A MONTH TILL THIS HERE THING BLOWS OVER ...

MEANWHILE ...

WHAT— WHAT HAPPENED? THAT HOLE ..FELL THROUGH.. AH, SPECTRE, YOU'RE NOT HURT! I GUESS I'M NOT EITHER, BONES SEEM TO BE ALL RIGHT, THIS SOFT EARTH MUST HAVE CUSHIONED OUR FALL.

AHA, I SEE! THEY MUST HAVE DUG THEIR TRAP RIGHT OVER A SECTION OF THIS ABANDONED MINE. THE FORCE OF OUR FALL CARRIED US RIGHT THROUGH INTO THE MINE ITSELF ...

IT'S DARK IN HERE — BUT WE SHALL SEE WHAT WE SHALL SEE...

AND AT THAT MOMENT ...
THAR! SEALED! WE'RE SNUG HERE! NOBODY KIN GIT IN! NOPE— NOT EVEN A GHOST!

SUCH A GREAT DEAL OF WORK! TSK! TSK! TSK! RUNNING AWAY FROM SOMEBODY?
THUH GHOST RIDER! YIIIII!

NOW YOU WILL FEEL THE WRATH OF THE GHOST RIDER!

THIS FOOD DIDN'T LAST AS LONG AS YOU EXPECTED, DID IT, CLASHER?

NOW THAT THIS IS OVER...

DIG!

THIS IS PROBABLY THE HARDEST DAY'S WORK YOU EVER DID IN YOUR LIVES.

BUT YOU'LL REST TONIGHT — IN JAIL! AND THAT MONEY YOU HAVE STOLEN WILL GO BACK TO THE MEN YOU STOLE IT FROM. YES, THERE WILL BE TIME FOR THINKING IN JAIL — THINK, THEN, ABOUT JUSTICE — AND ABOUT THE GHOST RIDER... HE WHO RIDES THE WINGS OF NIGHT!
THE END

THE HOLLOW MEN

A penny for the Old Guy

I

We are the hollow men
We are the stuffed men
Leaning together
Headpiece filled with straw. Alas!
Our dried voices, when
We whisper together
Are quiet and meaningless
As wind in dry grass
Or rats' feet over broken glass
In our dry cellar

Shape without form, shade without colour.
Paralysed force, gesture without motion;

Those who have crossed
With direct eyes, to death's other Kingdom
Remember us—if at all—not as lost
Violent souls, but only
As the hollow men

II

Eyes I dare not meet in dreams
In death's dream kingdom
These do not appear:
There, the eyes are
Sunlight on a broken column
There, is a tree swinging
And voices are
In the wind's singing
More distant and more solemn
Than a fading star.

Let me be no nearer
In death's dream kingdom
Let me also wear
Such deliberate disguises

Rat's coat, crowskin, crossed staves
In a field
Behaving as the wind behaves
No nearer—

Not that final meeting
In the twilight kingdom

This is the dead land
This is cactus land
Here the stone images
Are raised, here they receive
The supplication of a dead man's hand
Under the twinkle of a fading star.

Is it like this
In death's other kingdom
Waking alone
At the hour when we are
Trembling with tenderness
Lips that would kiss
Form prayers to broken stone.

IV

The eyes are not here
There are no eyes here
In this valley of dying stars
In this hollow valley
This broken jaw of our lost kingdoms

In this last of meeting places
We grope together
And avoid speech
Gathered on this beach of the tumid river

Sightless, unless
The eyes reappear
As the perpetual star
Multifoliate rose
Of death's twilight kingdom
The hope only
Of empty men.

V

Here we go round the prickly pear
Prickly pear prickly pear
Here we go round the prickly pear
At five o'clock in the morning.

Between the idea
And the reality
Between the motion
And the act
Falls the Shadow

For Thine is the Kingdom

Between the conception
And the creation
Between the emotion
And the response
Falls the Shadow

Life is very long

Between the desire
And the spasm
Between the potency
And the existence
Between the essence
And the descent
Falls the Shadow

For Thine is the Kingdom

For Thine is
Life is
For Thine is the

This is the way the world ends
This is the way the world ends
This is the way the world ends
Not with a bang but a whimper.

—T. S. Eliot, 1925

THE MASK

BY ROBERT W. CHAMBERS

Camilla: You, sir, should unmask.
Stranger: Indeed?
Cassilda: Indeed it's time. We have all laid
aside disguise but you.
Stranger: I wear no mask.
Camilla: (Terrified, aside to Cassilda) No
mask? No mask!
  — The King in Yellow, Act I, Scene 2.

1

ALTHOUGH I KNEW NOTHING OF CHEM-
istry, I listened fascinated. He picked
up an Easter lily which Geneviève
had brought that morning from Notre
Dame, and dropped it into the basin.
Instantly the liquid lost its crystalline
clearness. For a second the lily was envel-
oped in a milk-white foam, which disappeared, leaving the fluid opalescent.
Changing tints of orange and crimson
played over the surface, and then what
seemed to be a ray of pure sunlight
struck through from the bottom where
the lily was resting. At the same instant
he plunged his hand into the basin and
drew out the flower. "There is no danger," he explained, "if you choose the
right moment. That golden ray is the
signal."

He held the lily toward me, and I
took it in my hand. It had turned to
stone, to the purest marble.

"You see," he said, "it is without a
flaw. What sculptor could reproduce it?"

The marble was white as snow, but
in its depths the veins of the lily were
tinged with palest azure, and a faint
flush lingered deep in its heart.

"Don't ask me the reason of that,"
he smiled, noticing my wonder. "I have
no idea why the veins and heart are
tinted, but they always are. Yesterday
I tried one of Geneviève's gold-fish,—
there it is."

The fish looked as if sculptured in
marble. But if you held it to the light
the stone was beautifully veined with a
faint blue, and from somewhere within
came a rosy light like the tint which
slumbers in an opal. I looked into the
basin. Once more it seemed filled with
clearest crystal.

"If I should touch it now?" I
demanded.

"I don't know," he replied, "but you
had better not try."

"There is one thing I'm curious
about," I said, "and that is where the ray
of sunlight came from."

"It looked like a sunbeam true
enough," he said. "I don't know, it
always comes when I immerse any living thing. Perhaps," he continued, smiling, "perhaps it is the vital spark of the
creature escaping to the source from
whence it came."

I saw he was mocking, and threat-
ened him with a mahl-stick, but he only
laughed and changed the subject.

"Stay to lunch. Geneviève will be
here directly."

"I saw her going to early mass," I
said, "and she looked as fresh and sweet
as that lily—before you destroyed it."

"Do you think I destroyed it?" said
Boris gravely.

"Destroyed, preserved, how can we tell?"

We sat in the corner of a studio near his unfinished group of the "Fates." He leaned back on the sofa, twirling a sculptor's chisel and squinting at his work.

"By the way," he said, "I have finished pointing up that old academic Ariadne, and I suppose it will have to go to the Salon. It's all I have ready this year, but after the success the 'Madonna' brought me I feel ashamed to send a thing like that."

The "Madonna," an exquisite marble for which Geneviève had sat, had been the sensation of last year's Salon. I looked at the Ariadne. It was a magnificent piece of technical work, but I agreed with Boris that the world would expect something better of him than that. Still, it was impossible now to think of finishing in time for the Salon that splendid terrible group half shrouded in the marble behind me. The "Fates" would have to wait.

We were proud of Boris Yvain. We claimed him and he claimed us on the strength of his having been born in America, although his father was French and his mother was a Russian. Every one in the Beaux Arts called him Boris. And yet there were only two of us whom he addressed in the same familiar way—Jack Scott and myself.

Perhaps my being in love with Geneviève had something to do with his affection for me. Not that it had ever been acknowledged between us. But after all was settled, and she had told me with tears in her eyes that it was Boris whom she loved, I went over to his house and congratulated him. The perfect cordiality of that interview did not deceive either of us, I always believed, although to one at least it was a great comfort. I do not think he

and Geneviève ever spoke of the matter together, but Boris knew.

Geneviève was lovely. The Madonna-like purity of her face might have been inspired by the Sanctus in Gounod's Mass. But I was always glad when she changed that mood for what we called her "April Manœuvres." She was often as variable as an April day. In the morning grave, dignified and sweet, at noon laughing, capricious, at evening whatever one least expected. I preferred her so rather than in that Madonna-like tranquillity which stirred the depths of my heart. I was dreaming of Geneviève when he spoke again.

"What do you think of my discovery, Alec?"

"I think it wonderful."

"I shall make no use of it, you know, beyond satisfying my own curiosity so far as may be, and the secret will die with me."

"It would be rather a blow to sculpture, would it not? We painters lose more than we ever gain by photography."

Boris nodded, playing with the edge of the chisel.

"This new vicious discovery would corrupt the world of art. No, I shall never confide the secret to any one," he said slowly.

It would be hard to find any one less informed about such phenomena than myself; but of course I had heard of mineral springs so saturated with silica that the leaves and twigs which fell into them were turned to stone after a time. I dimly comprehended the process, how the silica replaced the vegetable matter, atom by atom, and the result was a duplicate of the object in stone. This, I confess, had never interested me greatly, and as for the ancient fossils thus produced, they disgusted me. Boris, it appeared, feeling curiosity instead of repugnance, had investigated the subject, and had accidentally stumbled on a solution which, attacking the immersed object with a ferocity unheard of, in a second did the work of years. This was all I could make out of the strange story he had just been telling me. He spoke again after a long silence.

"I am almost frightened when I think what I have found. Scientists would go mad over the discovery. It was so simple too; it discovered itself. When I think of that formula, and that new element precipitated in metallic scales—»

"What new element?"

"Oh, I haven't thought of naming it, and I don't believe I ever shall. There are enough precious metals now in the world to cut throats over."

I pricked up my ears. "Have you struck gold, Boris?"

"No, better;—but see here, Alec!" he laughed, starting up. "You and I have all we need in this world. Ah! how sinister and covetous you look already!" I laughed too, and told him I was devoured by the desire for gold, and we had better talk of something else; so when Geneviève came in shortly after, we had turned our backs on alchemy.

Geneviève was dressed in silvery grey from head to foot. The light glinted along the soft curves of her fair hair as she turned her cheek to Boris; then she saw me and returned my greeting. She had never before failed to blow me a kiss from the tips of her white fingers, and I promptly complained of the omission. She smiled and held out her hand, which dropped almost before it had touched mine; then she said, looking at Boris—

"You must ask Alec to stay for luncheon." This also was something new. She had always asked me herself until to-day.

"I did," said Boris shortly.

"And you said yes, I hope?" She turned to me with a charming conventional smile. I might have been an acquaintance of the day before yesterday. I made her a low bow. "J'avais bien l'honneur, madame," but refusing to take up our usual bantering tone, she murmured a hospitable commonplace and disappeared. Boris and I looked at one another.

"I had better go home, don't you think?" I asked.

"Hanged if I know," he replied frankly.

While we were discussing the advisability of my departure Geneviève reappeared in the doorway without her bonnet. She was wonderfully beautiful, but her colour was too deep and her lovely eyes were too bright. She came straight up to me and took my arm.

"Luncheon is ready. Was I cross, Alec? I thought I had a headache, but I haven't. Come here, Boris;" and she slipped her other arm through his. "Alec knows that after you there is no one in the world whom I like as well as I like him, so if he sometimes feels snubbed it won't hurt him."

«À la bonheur!" I cried, "who says there are no thunderstorms in April?"

"Are you ready?" chanted Boris. "Aye ready;" and arm-in-arm we raced into the dining-room, scandalizing the servants. After all we were not so much to blame; Geneviève was eighteen, Boris was twenty-three, and I not quite twenty-one.

II

SOME WORK THAT I WAS DOING ABOUT this time on the decorations for Geneviève's boudoir kept me constantly at the quaint little hotel in the Rue Sainte-Cécile. Boris and I in those days laboured hard but as we pleased, which was fitfully, and we all three, with Jack Scott, idled a great deal together.

One quiet afternoon I had been wandering alone over the house examining curios, prying into odd corners, bringing out sweetmeats and cigars from strange hiding-places, and at last I stopped in the bathing-room. Boris, all over clay, stood there washing his hands.

The room was built of rose-coloured marble excepting the floor, which was tessellated in rose and grey. In the centre was a square pool sunken below the surface of the floor; steps led down into it, sculptured pillars supported a frescoed ceiling. A delicious marble Cupid appeared to have just alighted on his pedestal at the upper end of the room. The whole interior was Boris' work and mine. Boris, in his working-clothes of white canvas, scraped the traces of clay and red modelling wax from his handsome hands, and coquetted over his shoulder with the Cupid.

"I see you," he insisted, "don't try to look the other way and pretend not to see me. You know who made you, little humbug!"

It was always my rôle to interpret Cupid's sentiments in these conversations, and when my turn came I responded in such a manner, that Boris seized my arm and dragged me toward the pool, declaring he would duck me. Next instant he dropped my arm and turned pale. "Good God!" he said, "I forgot the pool is full of the solution!"

I shivered a little, and dryly advised him to remember better where he had stored the precious liquid.

"In Heaven's name, why do you keep a small lake of that gruesome stuff here of all places?" I asked.

"I want to experiment on something large," he replied.

"On me, for instance?"

"Ah! that came too close for jesting; but I do want to watch the action of that solution on a more highly organized living body; there is that big white rabbit," he said, following me into the studio.

Jack Scott, wearing a paint-stained jacket, came wandering in, appropriated all the Oriental sweetmeats he could lay his hands on, looted the cigarette case, and finally he and Boris disappeared together to visit the Luxembourg Gallery, where a new silver bronze by Rodin and a landscape of Monet's were claiming the exclusive attention of artistic France. I went back to the studio, and resumed my work. It was a Renaissance screen, which Boris wanted me to paint for Geneviève's boudoir. But the small boy who was unwillingly dawdling through a series of poses for it, to-day refused all bribes to be good. He never rested an instant in the same position, and inside of five minutes I had as many different outlines of the little beggar.

"Are you posing, or are you executing a song and dance, my friend?" I inquired.

"Whichever monsieur pleases," he replied, with an angelic smile.

Of course I dismissed him for the day, and of course I paid him for the full time, that being the way we spoil our models.

After the young imp had gone, I made a few perfunctory daubs at my work, but was so thoroughly out of humour, that it took me the rest of the afternoon to undo the damage I had done, so at last I scraped my palette, stuck my brushes in a bowl of black soap, and strolled into the smoking-room. I really believe that, excepting Geneviève's apartments, no room in the house was so free from the perfume of tobacco as this one. It was a queer chaos of odds and ends, hung with threadbare tapestry. A sweet-toned old spinet in good repair stood by the window. There were stands of weapons, some old and dull, others bright and modern, festoons of Indian and Turkish armour over the mantel, two or three good pictures, and a pipe-rack. It was here that we used to come for new sensations in smoking. I doubt if any type of pipe ever existed which was not represented in that rack. When we had selected one, we immediately carried it somewhere else and smoked it; for the place was, on the whole, more gloomy and less inviting than any in the house. But this afternoon, the twilight was very soothing, the rugs and skins on the floor looked brown and soft and drowsy; the big couch was piled with cushions—I found my pipe and curled up there for an unaccustomed smoke in the smoking-room. I had chosen one with a long flexible stem, and lighting it fell to dreaming. After a while it went out, but I did not stir. I dreamed on and presently fell asleep.

I awoke to the saddest music I had ever heard. The room was quite dark, I had no idea what time it was. A ray of moonlight silvered one edge of the old spinet, and the polished wood seemed to exhale the sounds as perfume floats above a box of sandalwood. Some one rose in the darkness, and came away weeping quietly, and I was fool enough to cry out "Geneviève!»

She dropped at my voice, and, I had time to curse myself while I made a light and tried to raise her from the floor. She shrank away with a murmur of pain. She was very quiet, and asked for Boris. I carried her to the divan, and went to look for him, but he was not in the house, and the servants were gone to bed. Perplexed and anxious, I hurried back to Geneviève. She lay where I had left her, looking very white.

"I can't find Boris nor any of the servants," I said.

"I know," she answered faintly, "Boris has gone to Ept with Mr. Scott. I did not remember when I sent you for him just now."

"But he can't get back in that case before to-morrow afternoon, and—are you hurt? Did I frighten you into falling? What an awful fool I am, but I was only half awake."

"Boris thought you had gone home before dinner. Do please excuse us for letting you stay here all this time."

"I have had a long nap," I laughed, "so sound that I did not know whether I was still asleep or not when I found myself staring at a figure that was moving toward me, and called out your name. Have you been trying the old spinet? You must have played very softly."

I would tell a thousand more lies worse than that one to see the look of relief that came into her face. She smiled adorably, and said in her natural voice: "Alec, I tripped on that wolf's head, and I think my ankle is sprained. Please call Marie, and then go home."

I did as she bade me, and left her there when the maid came in.

III

At noon next day when I called, I found Boris walking restlessly about his studio.

"Geneviève is asleep just now," he told me, "the sprain is nothing, but why should she have such a high fever? The doctor can't account for it; or else he will not," he muttered.

"Geneviève has a fever?" I asked.

"I should say so, and has actually been a little light-headed at intervals all night. The idea!—gay little Geneviève, without a care in the world,—and she keeps saying her heart's broken, and she wants to die!"

My own heart stood still.

Boris leaned against the door of his studio, looking down, his hands in his pockets, his kind, keen eyes clouded, a new line of trouble drawn "over the mouth's good mark, that made the smile." The maid had orders to summon him the instant Geneviève opened her eyes. We waited and waited, and Boris, growing restless, wandered about, fussing with modelling wax and red clay. Suddenly he started for the next room. "Come and see my rose-coloured bath full of death!" he cried.

"Is it death?" I asked, to humour his mood.

"You are not prepared to call it life, I suppose," he answered. As he spoke he plucked a solitary gold-fish squirming and twisting out of its globe. "We'll send this one after the other—wherever that is," he said. There was feverish excitement in his voice. A dull weight of fever lay on my limbs and on my brain as I followed him to the fair crystal pool with its pink-tinted sides; and he dropped the creature in. Falling, its scales flashed with a hot orange gleam in its angry twistings and contortions; the moment it struck the liquid it became rigid and sank heavily to the bottom. Then came the milky foam, the splendid hues radiating on the surface and then the shaft of pure serene light broke through from seemingly infinite depths. Boris plunged in his hand and drew out an exquisite marble thing, blue-veined, rose-tinted, and glistening with opalescent drops.

"Child's play," he muttered, and looked wearily, longingly at me,—as if I could answer such questions! But Jack Scott came in and entered into the "game," as he called it, with ardour. Nothing would do but to try the experiment on the white rabbit then and there. I was willing that Boris should find distraction from his cares, but I hated to see the life go out of a warm, living creature and I declined to be present. Picking up a book at random, I sat down in the studio to read. Alas! I had found *The King in Yellow*. After a few moments, which seemed ages, I was putting it away with a nervous shudder, when Boris and Jack came in bringing their marble rabbit. At the same time the bell rang above, and a cry came from the sick-room. Boris was gone like a flash, and the next moment he called, "Jack, run for the doctor; bring him back with you. Alec, come here."

I went and stood at her door. A frightened maid came out in haste and ran away to fetch some remedy. Geneviève, sitting bolt upright, with crimson cheeks and glittering eyes, babbled incessantly and resisted Boris' gentle restraint. He called me to help. At my first touch she sighed and sank back, closing her eyes, and then—then—as we still bent above her, she opened them again, looked straight into Boris' face—poor fever-crazed girl!—and told her secret. At the same instant our three lives turned into new channels; the bond that held us so long together snapped for ever and a new bond was forged in its place, for she had spoken my name, and as the fever tortured her, her heart poured out its load of hidden sorrow. Amazed and dumb I bowed my head, while my face burned like a live coal, and the blood surged in my ears, stupefying me with its clamour. Incapable of movement, incapable of speech, I listened to her feverish words in an agony of shame and sorrow. I could not silence her, I could not look at Boris. Then I felt an arm upon my shoulder, and Boris turned a bloodless face to mine.

"It is not your fault, Alec; don't grieve so if she loves you—" but he could not finish; and as the doctor stepped swiftly into the room, saying—"Ah, the fever!" I seized Jack Scott and hurried him to the street, saying, "Boris would rather be alone." We crossed the street to our own apartments, and that night, seeing I was going to be ill too, he went for the doctor again. The last thing I recollect with any distinctness was hearing Jack say, "For Heaven's sake, doctor, what ails him, to wear a face like that?" and I thought of *The King in Yellow* and the Pallid Mask.

I was very ill, for the strain of two years which I had endured since that fatal May morning when Geneviève murmured, "I love you, but I think I love Boris best," told on me at last. I had never imagined that it could become more than I could endure. Outwardly tranquil, I had deceived myself. Although the inward battle raged night after night, and I, lying alone in my room, cursed myself for rebellious thoughts unloyal to Boris and unworthy of Geneviève, the morning always brought relief, and I returned to Geneviève and to my dear Boris with a heart washed clean by the tempests of the night.

Never in word or deed or thought while with them had I betrayed my sorrow even to myself.

The mask of self-deception was no longer a mask for me, it was a part of me. Night lifted it, laying bare the stifled truth below; but there was no one to see except myself, and when the day broke the mask fell back again of its own accord. These thoughts passed through my troubled mind as I lay sick, but they were hopelessly entangled with visions of white creatures, heavy as stone, crawling about in Boris' basin,— of the wolf's head on the rug, foaming and snapping at Geneviève, who lay smiling beside it. I thought, too, of the King in Yellow wrapped in the fantastic colours of his tattered mantle, and that bitter cry of Cassilda, "Not upon us, oh King, not upon us!" Feverishly I struggled to put it from me, but I saw the lake of Hali, thin and blank, without a ripple or wind to stir it, and I saw the towers of Carcosa behind the moon. Aldebaran, the Hyades, Alar, Hastur, glided through the cloud-rifts which fluttered and flapped as they passed like the scolloped tatters of the King in Yellow. Among all these, one sane thought persisted. It never wavered, no matter what else was going on in my disordered mind, that my chief reason for existing was to meet some requirement of Boris and Geneviève. What this obligation was, its nature, was never clear; sometimes it seemed to be protection, sometimes support, through a great crisis. Whatever it seemed to be for the time, its weight rested only on me, and I was never so ill or so weak that I did not respond with my whole soul. There were always crowds of faces about me, mostly strange, but a few I recognized, Boris among them. Afterward they told me that this could not have been, but I know that once at least he bent over me. It was only a touch, a faint echo of his voice, then the clouds settled back on my senses, and I lost him, but he *did* stand there and bend over me *once* at least.

At last, one morning I awoke to find the sunlight falling across my bed, and Jack Scott reading beside me. I had not strength enough to speak aloud, neither could I think, much less remember, but I could smile feebly, as Jack's eye met mine, and when he jumped up and asked eagerly if I wanted anything, I could whisper, "Yes—Boris." Jack moved to the head of my bed, and leaned down to arrange my pillow: I did not see his face, but he answered heartily, "You must wait, Alec; you are too weak to see even Boris."

I waited and I grew strong; in a few days I was able to see whom I would, but meanwhile I had thought and remembered. From the moment when all the past grew clear again in my mind, I never doubted what I should do when the time came, and I felt sure that Boris would have resolved upon the same course so far as he was concerned; as for what pertained to me alone, I knew he would see that also as I did. I no longer asked for any one. I never inquired why no message came from them; why during the week I lay there, waiting and growing stronger, I never heard their name spoken. Preoccupied with my own searchings for the right way, and with my feeble but determined fight against despair, I simply acquiesced in Jack's reticence, taking for granted that he was afraid to speak of them, lest I should turn unruly and insist on seeing them. Meanwhile I said over and over to myself, how would it be when life began again for us all? We would take up our relations exactly as they were before Geneviève fell ill. Boris and I would look into each other's eyes, and there would be neither rancour nor cowardice nor mistrust in that glance. I would be with them again for a little while in the dear intimacy of their home, and then, without pretext or explanation, I would disappear from their lives for ever. Boris would know; Geneviève—the only comfort was that she would never know. It seemed, as I thought it over, that I had found the meaning of that sense of obligation which had persisted all through my delirium, and the only possible answer to it. So, when I was quite ready, I beckoned Jack to me one day, and said—

"Jack, I want Boris at once; and take my dearest greeting to Geneviève...."

When at last he made me understand that they were both dead, I fell into a wild rage that tore all my little convalescent strength to atoms. I raved and cursed myself into a relapse, from which I crawled forth some weeks afterward a boy of twenty-one who believed that his youth was gone for ever. I seemed to be past the capability of further suffering, and one day when Jack handed me a letter and the keys to Boris' house, I took them without a tremor and asked him to tell me all. It was cruel of me to ask him, but there was no help for it, and he leaned wearily on his thin hands, to reopen the wound which could never entirely heal. He began very quietly—

"Alec, unless you have a clue that I know nothing about, you will not be able to explain any more than I what has happened. I suspect that you would rather not hear these details, but you must learn them, else I would spare you the relation. God knows I wish I could be spared the telling. I shall use few words.

"That day when I left you in the doctor's care and came back to Boris, I found him working on the 'Fates.' Geneviève, he said, was sleeping under the influence of drugs. She had been quite out of her mind, he said. He kept on working, not talking any more, and I watched him. Before long, I saw that the third figure of the group—the one looking straight ahead, out over the world—bore his face; not as you ever saw it, but as it looked then and to the end. This is one thing for which I should like to find an explanation, but I never shall.

"Well, he worked and I watched him in silence, and we went on that way until nearly midnight. Then we heard the door open and shut sharply, and a swift rush in the next room. Boris sprang through the doorway and I followed; but we were too late. She lay at the bottom of the pool, her hands across her breast. Then Boris shot himself through the heart." Jack stopped speaking, drops of sweat stood under his eyes, and his thin cheeks twitched. "I carried Boris to his room. Then I went back and let that hellish fluid out of the pool, and turning on all the water, washed the marble clean of every drop. When at length I dared descend the steps, I found her lying there as white as snow. At last, when I had decided what was best to do, I went into the laboratory, and first emptied the solution in the basin into the waste-pipe; then I poured the contents of every jar and bottle after it. There was wood in the fireplace, so I built a fire, and breaking the locks of Boris' cabinet I burnt every paper, notebook and letter that I found there. With a mallet from the studio I smashed to pieces all the empty bottles, then loading them into a coal-scuttle, I carried them to the cellar and threw them over the red-hot bed of the furnace. Six times I made the journey, and at last, not a vestige remained of anything which might again aid in seeking for the formula which Boris had found. Then at last I dared call the doctor. He is a good man, and together we struggled to keep it from the public. Without him I never could have succeeded. At last we got the servants paid and sent away into the country, where old Rosier keeps them quiet with stories of Boris' and Geneviève's travels in distant lands, from whence they will not return

for years. We buried Boris in the little cemetery of Sèvres. The doctor is a good creature, and knows when to pity a man who can bear no more. He gave his certificate of heart disease and asked no questions of me."

Then, lifting his head from his hands, he said, "Open the letter, Alec; it is for us both."

I tore it open. It was Boris' will dated a year before. He left everything to Geneviève, and in case of her dying childless, I was to take control of the house in the Rue Sainte-Cécile, and Jack Scott the management at Ept. On our deaths the property reverted to his mother's family in Russia, with the exception of the sculptured marbles executed by himself. These he left to me.

The page blurred under our eyes, and Jack got up and walked to the window. Presently he returned and sat down again. I dreaded to hear what he was going to say, but he spoke with the same simplicity and gentleness.

"Geneviève lies before the Madonna in the marble room. The Madonna bends tenderly above her, and Geneviève smiles back into that calm face that never would have been except for her."

His voice broke, but he grasped my hand, saying, "Courage, Alec." Next morning he left for Ept to fulfil his trust.

IV

THE SAME EVENING I took the keys and went into the house I had known so well. Everything was in order, but the silence was terrible. Though I went twice to the door of the marble room, I could not force myself to enter. It was beyond my strength. I went into the smoking-room and sat down before the spinet. A small lace handkerchief lay on the keys, and I turned away, choking. It was plain I could not stay, so I locked every door, every window, and the three front and back gates, and went away. Next morning Alcide packed my valise, and leaving him in charge of my apartments I took the Orient express for Constantinople. During the two years that I wandered through the East, at first, in our letters, we never mentioned Geneviève and Boris, but gradually their names crept in. I recollect particularly a passage in one of Jack's letters replying to one of mine—

"What you tell me of seeing Boris bending over you while you lay ill, and feeling his touch on your face, and hearing his voice, of course troubles me. This that you describe must have happened a fortnight after he died. I say to myself that you were dreaming, that it was part of your delirium, but the explanation does not satisfy me, nor would it you."

Toward the end of the second year a letter came from Jack to me in India so unlike anything that I had ever known of him that I decided to return at once to Paris. He wrote: "I am well, and sell all my pictures as artists do who have no need of money. I have not a care of my own, but I am more restless than if I had. I am unable to shake off a strange anxiety about you. It is not apprehension, it is rather a breathless expectancy—of what, God knows! I can only say it is wearing me out. Nights I dream always of you and Boris. I can never recall anything afterward, but I wake in the morning with my heart beating, and all day the excitement increases until I fall asleep at night to recall the same experience. I am quite exhausted by it, and have determined to break up this morbid condition. I must see you. Shall I go to Bombay, or will you come to Paris?"

I telegraphed him to expect me by the next steamer.

When we met I thought he had changed very little; I, he insisted, looked in splendid health. It was good to hear his voice again, and as we sat and chatted about what life still held for us, we felt that it was pleasant to be alive in the bright spring weather.

We stayed in Paris together a week, and then I went for a week to Ept with him, but first of all we went to the cemetery at Sèvres, where Boris lay.

"Shall we place the 'Fates' in the little grove above him?" Jack asked, and I answered—

"I think only the 'Madonna' should watch over Boris' grave." But Jack was none the better for my home-coming. The dreams of which he could not retain even the least definite outline continued, and he said that at times the sense of breathless expectancy was suffocating.

"You see I do you harm and not good," I said. "Try a change without me." So he started alone for a ramble among the Channel Islands, and I went back to Paris. I had not yet entered Boris' house, now mine, since my return, but I knew it must be done. It had been kept in order by Jack; there were servants there, so I gave up my own apartment and went there to live. Instead of the agitation I had feared, I found myself able to paint there tranquilly. I visited all the rooms—all but one. I could not bring myself to enter the marble room where Geneviève lay, and yet I felt the longing growing daily to look upon her face, to kneel beside her.

One April afternoon, I lay dreaming in the smoking-room, just as I had lain two years before, and mechanically

I looked among the tawny Eastern rugs for the wolf-skin. At last I distinguished the pointed ears and flat cruel head, and I thought of my dream where I saw Geneviève lying beside it. The helmets still hung against the threadbare tapestry, among them the old Spanish morion which I remembered Geneviève had once put on when we were amusing ourselves with the ancient bits of mail. I turned my eyes to the spinet; every yellow key seemed eloquent of her caressing hand, and I rose, drawn by the strength of my life's passion to the sealed door of the marble room. The heavy doors swung inward under my trembling hands. Sunlight poured through the window, tipping with gold the wings of Cupid, and lingered like a nimbus over the brows of the Madonna. Her tender face bent in compassion over a marble form so exquisitely pure that I knelt and signed myself. Geneviève lay in the shadow under the Madonna, and yet, through her white arms, I saw the pale azure vein, and beneath her softly clasped hands the folds of her dress were tinged with rose, as if from some faint warm light within her breast.

Bending, with a breaking heart, I touched the marble drapery with my lips, then crept back into the silent house.

A maid came and brought me a letter, and I sat down in the little conservatory to read it; but as I was about to break the seal, seeing the girl lingering, I asked her what she wanted.

She stammered something about a white rabbit that had been caught in the house, and asked what should be done with it. I told her to let it loose in the walled garden behind the house, and opened my letter. It was from Jack, but so incoherent that I thought he must have lost his reason. It was nothing but a series of prayers to me not to leave the house until he could get back; he could not tell me why, there were the dreams, he said—he could explain nothing, but he was sure that I must not leave the house in the Rue Sainte-Cécile.

As I finished reading I raised my eyes and saw the same maid-servant standing in the doorway holding a glass dish in which two gold-fish were swimming: "Put them back into the tank and tell me what you mean by interrupting me," I said.

With a half-suppressed whimper she emptied water and fish into an aquarium at the end of the conservatory, and turning to me asked my permission to leave my service. She said people were playing tricks on her, evidently with a design of getting her into trouble; the marble rabbit had been stolen and a live one had been brought into the house; the two beautiful marble fish were gone, and she had just found those common live things flopping on the dining-room floor. I reassured her and sent her away, saying I would look about myself. I went into the studio; there was nothing there but my canvases and some casts, except the marble of the Easter lily. I saw it on a table across the room. Then I strode angrily over to it. But the flower I lifted from the table was fresh and fragile and filled the air with perfume.

Then suddenly I comprehended, and sprang through the hallway to the marble room. The doors flew open, the sunlight streamed into my face, and through it, in a heavenly glory, the Madonna smiled, as Geneviève lifted her flushed face from her marble couch and opened her sleepy eyes.

THE END

"WRITING A BOOK IS A HORRIBLE, EXHAUSTING STRUGGLE, LIKE A LONG BOUT WITH SOME PAINFUL ILLNESS. ONE WOULD NEVER UNDERTAKE SUCH A THING IF ONE WERE NOT DRIVEN ON BY SOME DEMON WHOM ONE CAN NEITHER RESIST NOR UNDERSTAND."

— GEORGE ORWELL

"AS FOR LITERARY CRITICISM IN GENERAL: I HAVE LONG FELT THAT ANY REVIEWER WHO EXPRESSES RAGE AND LOATHING FOR A NOVEL OR A PLAY OR A POEM IS PREPOSTEROUS. HE OR SHE IS LIKE A PERSON WHO HAS PUT ON FULL ARMOR AND ATTACKED A HOT FUDGE SUNDAE OR A BANANA SPLIT."

— KURT VONNEGUT JR.

MOBY DICK
Adapted from the book by HERMAN MELVILLE

Chapter 1. BEWARE OF CAPTAIN AHAB!

ONLY ONE MAN SURVIVED TO TELL THE STORY OF MOBY DICK'S REVENGE.

THIS MAN WAS A SCHOOLMASTER. TALL AND DARK-HAIRED HE WAS, BROAD OF SHOULDER AND RUDDY OF COMPLEXION, BELYING HIS GENTLE PROFESSION WITH A PAIR OF SEA-BLUE EYES — THE EYES OF A BORN SEAMAN.

HIS NAME WAS ISHMAEL.

AT THE TIME THIS STRANGE AND THRILLING STORY OPENS, ISHMAEL, HAVING LITTLE MONEY IN HIS POCKET AND NO SCHOOL IN WHICH TO TEACH, DECIDED TO SEE SOMETHING OF THE WORLD — *THE WORLD OF WATER THAT LAY BEYOND AMERICA'S ATLANTIC SEABOARD...*

THE INN PARLOUR WAS PACKED WITH SEAMEN AND THICK WITH SMOKE AND THE TARRY SMELL OF DAMP OILSKINS — ISHMAEL APPROACHED THE ONE-ARMED INNKEEPER . . .
HAVE YOU A ROOM FOR THE NIGHT, A SUPPER, AND A BITE FOR TOMORROW'S BREAKFAST ?
AYE, MATEY — IF YOU AIN'T NO OBJECTION TO SHARING A HARPOONER'S BLANKET.

A PLATE OF HOT DUMPLINGS WAS SET BEFORE THE SEAFARING SCHOOLMASTER .
THIS HARPOONER YOU SPOKE OF —
HEH ! A DARK-COMPLEXIONED CHAP, HE IS , MAHOGANY DARK , EATS NOTHING BUT STEAKS AND LIKES 'EM RAW. HE'LL BE HERE AFORE LONG — THAT IS , IF HE'S MANAGED TO SELL HIS HEAD !

SELL HIS HEAD? ARE YOU TELLING ME THAT A STEAK-EATING, DARK-VISAGED HARPOONER IS ACTUALLY ENGAGED, THIS VERY SUNDAY NIGHT OF ALL NIGHTS, IN PEDDLING HIS HEAD AROUND THE TOWN?
NOT HIS OWN HEAD, BLESS YOU! AN EMBALMED NEW ZEALAND HEAD — GREAT CURIOS THEY ARE — HE'S SOLD 'EM ALL BUT ONE — PEDDLES 'EM ROUND THE STREETS LIKE ONIONS ON A STRING — A RARE FELLER HE IS!

ISHMAEL WAS LATER SHOWN TO HIS ROOM. THERE HE STRETCHED HIMSELF OUT ON THE MATTRESS . . .
THAT HARPOONER WILL BE A STRANGE BED MATE BY ALL ACCOUNTS. HEAVEN PRESERVE ME IF HE TAKES A FANCY TO MY HEAD!

TOWARDS MIDNIGHT, THE DOOR CREAKED OPEN . . . ISHMAEL AWOKE . . .
WHO'S THERE?

A FACE APPEARED IN THE LAMPLIGHT... AND SUCH A FACE! DARK IN COLOUR AND TATTOOED ALL OVER WITH BLACKISH DOTS IN CURIOUS PATTERNS. TEETH FILED TO POINTS LIKE THE FANGS OF A CIVET CAT. HEAD SHAVEN SAVE FOR A SAVAGE TUFT TWISTED UP WITH A SCALP KNOT!
HEAVEN SMITE ME BLIND. SO THAT I MAY NEVER BEHOLD THE LIKE AGAIN!

WITH AN ANIMAL-LIKE SNARL, THE UNEARTHLY NEWCOMER LEAPED AT ISHMAEL ... AND THE GLITTERING POINT OF A HARPOON SPEAR HOVERED MENACINGLY AN INCH FROM THE SCHOOLMASTER-SEAMAN'S BARE CHEST!
NNNNNNGAH! WHO—A—YOU? YOU NO SPEAKEE, ME KILLEE!
FRIEND! ME FRIEND! I ASSURE YOU!

JUST AT THAT MOMENT, THE INNKEEPER PUT HIS HEAD IN THE DOORWAY, AND THE SAVAGE LOWERED HIS WEAPON WITH A HAPPY GRIN...
GO SLEEPEE QUEEQUEG! YOU KEEPEE ALL PEOPLES AWAKEE. THIS FELLER HE SLEEPEE YOU. HIM GOOD FELLER!
GOOD FELLER! WAUGH! QUEEQUEG PLENTY FRIENDEE ALL GOOD FELLER!

SUCH WAS ISHMAEL'S INTRODUCTION TO QUEEQUEG, THE HALF-WILD NEW ZEALAND HARPOONER WHO WAS TO BECOME HIS STAUNCH FRIEND AND SHIPMATE IN UNHEARD-OF PERILS.
NEXT MORNING AFTER A SOUND NIGHT'S SLEEP, THE LANDLORD TOLD HIM OF QUEEQUEG'S PROWESS AS THEY SAT AT BREAKFAST...
HE WAS A PRINCE AMONGST HIS OWN PEOPLE SO THEY SAY. NOW HE'S THE BEST HARPOONER WHO EVER FLUNG IRON INTO A WHALE'S BACK. IF YOU WAS LOOKIN' FOR A SHIP, MATEY, YOU COULDN'T DO BETTER THAN GO ALONGER QUEEQUEG. HE'S BOUND FOR NANTUCKET TO FIND HIMSELF A BERTH IN A WHALING SHIP.
A WHALING SHIP! I'LL LET FATE GUIDE ME, A WHALING SHIP IT SHALL BE!

NANTUCKET IN 1841 WAS THE CENTRE OF A GREAT WHALING INDUSTRY.
TALL SCHOONERS, REEKING OF MAMMAL OIL, PACKED THE BUSY QUAYS.
EVERYWHERE WERE WHALING MEN OF THE NANTUCKET BREED.
TALL MEN—MEN WITH FEARLESS, FAR-OFF EYES— MEN MORE USED
TO THE WILDERNESS OF THE SPUME-FLUNG OCEAN THAN THE CROWDED
WHARVES OF THEIR HOME PORT, DEARLY THOUGH THEY LOVED IT...
SO IT WAS THAT ISHMAEL AND QUEEQUEG CAME TO NANTUCKET...
WHAT'S THAT INFERNAL THING YOU HAVE IN YOUR HAND, QUEEQUEG? AN EBONY IDOL!
THISEE YO-JO! HIM POWERFUL FELLER... YO-JO SPEAKEE QUEEQUEG... HIM SAY TELLEE FRIEND GO FINDEE SHIP... ANY SHIP... THEN WE GO SAIL IN SHIP 'COS HIM BE GOOD SHIP YOU BET!

ISHMAEL GAZED IN ASTONISHMENT AT THE GRINNING HARPOONER . . .
YOU WANT ME TO CHOOSE OUR SHIP ? BUT, QUEEQUEG, I KNOW NOTHING OF THE WHALING BUSINESS — I WAS RELYING ON YOUR JUDGEMENT !
YO-JO SPEAKEE QUEEQUEG . . . FRIEND GO FINDEE SHIP— HIM BE GOOD SHIP, YOU BET !

QUEEQUEG WOULD BROOK NO ARGUMENT . HE PERSISTED IN HIS BELIEF THAT GOOD FORTUNE WOULD FOLLOW IF THEY OBEYED THE "ORDERS" OF THE LITTLE EBONY IDOL.
. . . SO ISHMAEL WALKED, ALONE, DOWN THE SHIP-LINED QUAY . . .
HERE'S A PRETTY TASK , TO CHOOSE FROM AMONGST ALL THESE FINE VESSELS . SHALL IT BE THE TIT-BIT , OR THE SALAMANDER , THE OJIBWAY , OR THE PEQUOD ?

ACTING UPON AN IMPULSE, ISHMAEL STRODE UP THE GANGPLANK OF THE "PEQUOD" WHERE HE FOUND A SEVERE-LOOKING MAN IN QUAKER BLUE STANDING NEAR THE QUARTER-DECK RAIL . . .
DO YOU NEED TWO EXTRA HANDS, CAPTAIN ? A SEAMAN OF SOME EXPERIENCE — AND A FINE HARPOONER ?
I AM NOT THE CAPTAIN OF THE PEQUOD, BOY — MY NAME IS PELEG AND I OWN HALF OF HER. CAPTAIN AHAB IS HER MASTER — HAST THOU CLAPPED EYES ON HIM ?

ISHMAEL EXPLAINED THAT HE AND HIS COMRADE HAD ONLY JUST ARRIVED IN NANTUCKET . . .
THOU WILT FIND CAPTAIN AHAB A STERN AND GOD-FEARING MASTER, BOY — THOU WILT FIND THAT HE HAS ONLY ONE LEG, THE OTHER HAVING BEEN DEVOURED, CHEWED UP, CRUNCHED BY THE MONSTROUSEST SPERM WHALE THAT EVER STOVE A BOAT — SHOULDEST THOU STILL FEEL INCLINED FOR WHALING, COME ABOARD ON THE MORROW WITH THY GEAR ; FAREWELL TO THEE NOW, I HAVE BUSINESS NEEDING MY ATTENTION !

ISHMAEL AND THE TATTOOED HARPOONER REPAIRED ABOARD THE "PEQUOD" NEXT MORNING. CAPTAIN PELEG WAS ON DECK AND HE REACTED VIOLENTLY TO THE SIGHT OF QUEEQUEG . . .
AAAAH! A HEATHEN! SHALL A HEATHEN TREAD THE DECK OF THIS GOD-FEARING SHIP?
QUEEQUEG IS A HARPOONER TO BE RECKONED WITH, SIR, FOR ALL HIS APPEARANCE
WAUGH! LOOKEE SEE CAP'AIN! YOU LOOKEE SEE!
LEAPING TO THE BULWARKS, QUEEQUEG BRACED HIS LEFT KNEE AND POISED HIS HARPOON . . .
CAP'AIN! YOU SEE HIM SMALL DROP TAR FLOATEE ON WATER DERE? YOU SEE HIM? WELL, S'POSE HIM ONE WHALE EYE, WELL, DEN?
FOR A HARPOONER TO STRIKE THAT SMALL DROP OF TAR FLOATING IN THE WATER, 'TWOULD INDEED BE WORTH OVERLOOKING HIS HEATHENISH QUALITY!

WHOOOOSH! SMACK! STRAIGHT AND TRUE, THE DEADLY WEAPON SLASHED DOWNWARDS — AND STRUCK THE SPOT OF FLOATING TAR FAIR AND SQUARE!
YEEEEEH! S'POSE HIM WHALE EYE — WHY DAT WHALE DEAD!
HEATHEN! HENCEFORTH, THOU ART A HARPOONER OF THE PEQUOD!

REJOICING AT THEIR GOOD FORTUNE IN SECURING BERTHS SO EASILY, THE TWO COMRADES WENT FOR A STROLL ALONG THE QUAY SIDE, THE "PEQUOD" BEING DUE TO SAIL ON THE NEXT TIDE. IT WAS THEN THAT THEY ENCOUNTERED THE SHABBY STRANGER WITH THE POCK-MARKED FACE...
HEY! MATEYS — HAVE YE SHIPPED IN THAT SHIP? TELL ME NO FOR THE GOOD O' YOUR SOULS!
AWAY WITH YOU, FELLOW — YOU MUST BE CRAZED!

IGNORING THE REBUFF, THE WILD-EYED MAN FOLLOWED THEM, PAWING AT ISHMAEL'S SLEEVE...
HAVE YE SEEN OLD THUNDER YET? HAVE YE SEEN CAP'N AHAB? HAS HE TOLD YOU HIS SECRET? HAS HE TOLD YOU WHAT HE'S ABOUT?
SECRET? WHAT SECRET IS THIS OF CAPTAIN AHAB'S?

THE POCK-MARKED MAN STEPPED BACK—NERVOUSLY, HIS TALON-LIKE HANDS CLUTCHED AT THE WALL BEHIND HIM — AND HIS VOICE BURST FROM HIS LIPS IN A CHOKED HOARSE WHISPER...
BEWARE O' CAP'N AHAB! WHAT'S TO BE MUST BE, AN' I RECKON SOME SAILORS OR OTHER MUST GO WITH HIM, AS WELL YE AS ANY OTHER MEN — BUT FOR THE GOOD O' YOUR SOULS, I WARN YE — BEWARE O' CAP'N AHAB AN' ALL HIS WORKS!
WITH THESE FORBIDDING WORDS, THE SHABBY STRANGER TURNED, AND WAS GONE!

CONTRIBUTORS

MICHAEL BUNKER is a *USA Today* Bestselling author, off-gridder, husband, and father of four children. He lives with his family in Central Texas where he reads and writes books…and occasionally tilts at windmills. In November of 2015, Variety Magazine announced that Michael had sold a film/tv option for his bestselling novel *Pennsylvania* to Jorgensen Pictures.

WILLIAM E. B. DU BOIS (1868 – 1963) was an American sociologist, socialist, historian, and Pan-Africanist civil rights activist.

ROBERT W. CHAMBERS (1865 – 1933) was an American artist and fiction writer, best known for his book of short stories titled *The King in Yellow*.

T. S. ELIOT (1888 – 1965) was a poet, essayist and playwright.[1] He is considered to be one of the 20th century's greatest poets, as well as a central figure in English-language Modernist poetry.

E. M. FORSTER (1879 – 1970) was an English author, best known for his novels, particularly *A Room with a View*, *Howards End*, and *A Passage to India*.

GARDNER FOX (1911 – 1986) was an American writer known best for creating numerous comic book characters for DC Comics. He is estimated to have written more than 4,000 comics stories,[4] including 1,500 for DC Comics. Fox was also a science fiction author and wrote many novels and short stories.

HERMAN MELVILLE (1819 – 1891) was an American novelist, short story writer, and poet of the American Renaissance period. Among his best-known works are *Moby-Dick*, *Typee,* and *Billy Budd, Sailor*. At the time of his death, Melville was no longer well known to the public, but the 1919 centennial of his birth was the starting point of a Melville revival. *Moby-Dick* eventually would be considered one of the great American novels.

KEVIN G. SUMMERS is the author of *Legendarium*, *The Man Who Shot John Wilkes Booth*, and *The Bleak December*.

BOOTH TARKINGTON (1869 – 1946) was an American novelist and dramatist best known for his novels The Magnificent Ambersons (1918) and Alice Adams (1921). He is one of only four novelists to win the Pulitzer Prize for Fiction more than once.

MARV WOLFMAN is an American comic book and novelization writer. He worked on Marvel Comics's *The Tomb of Dracula*, for which he and artist Gene Colan created the vampire-slayer *Blade*, and DC Comics's *The New Teen Titans* and the *Crisis on Infinite Earths* limited series with George Pérez.

www.ingramcontent.com/pod-product-compliance
Lightning Source LLC
Chambersburg PA
CBHW080841160726

47999CB00009B/2965